To all those who gave me a hand along the way, thanks. You know who you are.

To Zabrina, my everlasting love and gratitude.

"Sacrifice is a part of life. It's supposed to be. It's not something to regret. It's something to aspire to."

— Mitch Albom, The Five People You Meet in Heaven

Foreword

PROLOGUES, SOME SAY, have become outdated. That may be the case, but for you, the reader, I do feel it is essential you are aware of something of the background to this story. That background is set out here in the foreword and preface.

I penned a UK bestselling memoir, 'Undercover: Operation Julie - The Inside Story.' It tells the tale of my role as one of only four undercover detectives on what is still one of the world's largest drug busts. It was pioneering work and is still a point of reference today for all British covert policing and training of undercover operatives.

In that book, I write about uncovering a huge plot to import massive quantities of cocaine into Britain from Bolivia via Miami back in the 1970s. The two people involved in that conspiracy were known to me as Bill and Blue. They were never arrested by the British police. But I was told by my former operational boss, Dick Lee, that they had been arrested by the Drug Enforcement Agency (DEA), a branch of American federal law enforcement. I was further informed they ended up doing serious time in a federal penitentiary.

I always had my doubts about who Bill and Blue really were. Were they "bad guys" or something completely different? It is that question that inspired me to write this book. Please remember, what you are about to read is fiction. None of the characters are real. The question has been in my mind for many years. What follows is a figment of my imagination with one proviso - the episode you will read, about what happened in Liverpool and the journey back to Wales is real, save for some adaption and minor changes for literary reasons. I transplanted it from my memoir as it serves a useful introduction to all the main characters including undercover cop, Steve Regan.

The opening chapters take place in September 1976. The chapters following that take place before and after that time. I have indicated the timeline at the start of a chapter where I felt it would help you, the reader, to follow the timeline.

Steve Regan is not me! Red is not my undercover buddy on Operation Julie. I have not got a clue who the real Bill and Blue were; they are not the characters of the same name in this novel. Caroline Sewell and Callum Colhoun are fictitious and bear no resemblance to any of the barristers I knew during my days at London's Criminal Bar - well, only small bits.

Before I start my story, please allow me to say this: As far as I am aware this book is unique in British literature. It is the first work of crime fiction about an undercover cop written by a former undercover cop. Please correct me if I am wrong.

Preface

THE FOLLOWING STORY is set in 1976. Back then, few people knew of the existence of GCHQ. Perhaps some vaguely knew it had connections to Bletchley Park and the cracking of the Enigma Code during World War Two. The end of that war saw the beginnings of the Cold War. It is then that the work of GCHQ expanded.

GCHQ, as the Government Communications Headquarters is better known, is housed in Cheltenham, Gloucestershire, England. Most people know it as the eyes and ears of the United Kingdom government. Some know it as "spooksville," using the Americanism of "spook" rather than the British "spy." It employs "spies in the sky" as well as other sophisticated eavesdropping devices to monitor activities deemed to be injurious to the state or its allies. Its work, of necessity, is shrouded in secrecy.

What is not generally known is this organisation is also tasked with assisting in intelligence gathering to combat serious organised crime. Just like invisible eyes and ears, it oversees many law enforcement activities including police and Customs undercover operations. It oversees in the sense it watches and listens, and gathers intelligence. To be precise, one department holds this brief – the Composite Signals Organisation (CSO).

The employees at GCHQ may as well have no name. They are faceless civil servants, UK government employees. They are not spies nor are they law enforcement officers. Some, like an anonymous middle-aged man I will call Jack, are frustrated cops. They see and hear of the exciting adrenaline fuelled lives of the men and women in the field. They marvel at the skills deployed by the undercover operatives living duplicitous lives and the inherent danger they place themselves in. Jack was fascinated by all of that. Jack knew he was good at his job within CSO and was content to play a role in the fight against crime and terrorism; a desk bound role that fulfilled him until he heard some terrible news from an old friend.

Chapter 1

THE CANADIAN COULD be an assassin. For sure, a big player dealing in vast quantities of heroin and cocaine. Bolivia is the source of the cocaine powder. It arrived into his control in an almost one hundred percent form. By the time it reached the streets of London it became a changed beast. If lucky, you may have had a purity of forty-five percent.

He did not control the chain of distribution all the way to street-level dealers. No need for that. Way too risky and more importantly, by the time he sold a one-pound 'weight' to Steve Regan, he had made a handsome profit.

Regan is the British man talking to the Canadian in a Liverpool nightclub in 1976. Coke, charlie or snow, to use some of its names, remained the preserve of the wealthy in 1976. Expensive, but popular with rock stars. A massive market and a huge opportunity for profit existed in Britain.

The deal had been laid out on the table. The Canadian and Regan became parties to a conspiracy to import serious weights of cocaine into Britain.

The Canadian's mood changed. Why? Not clear to Regan at all. Without him revealing too many details, the Canadian had impressed with the plan.

- Bolivia – check!
- Go-fast boat in place – check!
- Air hostess to bring the contraband into Britain – check!

• Prices and discounts for quantity – check!

Snap! The mood did change, and how!

"Are you guys cops?"

Wham! This question hit Regan like a vivid lightning strike from a clear blue sky. The words rolled around inside his head like thunderclaps.

A simulated assassination followed. A double-tap from a silenced semi-automatic pistol favoured by professional hitmen the world over. A close-range execution.

He raised one hand next to Regan's head. The Canadian pointed his joined forefinger and middle finger in imitating a gun. The fingers touched Regan's skin.

He silently mouthed the silenced spitting sound as two imaginary shells splattered Regan's brains out of the gaping exit wounds at the far side of his head.

Pop! Pop!

This is personal, thought Regan.

WELCOME TO STEVE REGAN'S world, the world of an undercover cop, identity confusion; a world with the slimmest of hold on reality or his true identity. He moves chameleon-like in the underworld mixing with those who inhabit dark places.

He is a man more likely to say, "Who the fuck am I?" when catching his reflection in a mirror, and most unlikely to utter a polite, "who am I?"

Chapter 2

LIVERPOOL, ENGLAND, September 1976

REGAN HAD DOZED ON the long journey to Liverpool. He snoozed, no more than a cat nap. Who the fuck am I? was the theme of his dream fuelled by identity confusion. He also had a fear of talking in his sleep. Undercover cop Steve Regan trusted his partner with his life and was further relaxed knowing Red knew how to drive well – funny how good drivers have a sixth sense. Knowing he was safe with him, Regan dozed. He dreamed. Regan dreamed of people in his secret real world. He dreamed about his sick mother and his wife and daughter.

There was one other man in the vehicle besides Regan and Red. He was called Blue. He looked like a hippie and wore a leather Stetson hat. Little did Regan know how things would turn out at the end of this journey. He had no idea that in just a few hours a cold-eyed mobster would threaten his life. Regan possessed a quickness of thoughts and an uncanny ability to smell trouble. This time, Regan's sixth sense did not see the threat coming.

The noise of a car horn woke Regan. Through half-closed eyes he saw the Jaguar overtake the van. What a beautiful machine! Sleek, powerful and sexy! My police pay could never afford one of those. Those kind of thoughts were a recurring theme for him.

Steve Regan was not his real name. That was the name on his fake driving licence, a part of his legend, or backstory. Red drove an old blue van, also part of the legend with a ghost registration.

The Jaguar pulled into a gravelled drive and crunched to a halt outside a large, white two-storey detached house. As they drove by, Regan noticed long slender legs swing out from the driver's side. She had beautiful blonde hair blowing in the breeze. He felt envious. I bet her old man is a drug dealer. Why can't I meet a rich, good-looking blonde? Fleeting thoughts, and he fell asleep again. He dreamed of money, and fears of turning into a dishonest rogue cop if offered the right drugs deal. As soon as he went through that nightmare scene, he relaxed knowing it could never happen with Red by his side, dependable, solid Red.

Regan loved the thrill of undercover work. It freed him from the tedious paperwork of ordinary police activity. It also distanced him from the petty bureaucracy of the ordinary police world, a world of 'everything in triplicate.' It was also a world of not 'bucking the system.' He had grown weary of asking why certain things were done that way. He grew even more weary of the answer, "Because we have always done it that way." Those irritations maddened Regan and other free spirits like him. Regan detested 'playing the game.' Particularly when the game was self-defeating. As a young detective, he could not fathom the sense in 'cuffing crime.' He soon learned to 'cuff a crime' was to fail to record it because it screwed up the detection rate stats. Regan could not see the sense in that. They were overworked as detectives and needed manpower. Why manipulate the figures to show less crime? Less crime meant fewer detectives. Regan soon found it was better to use his intellect fighting crime rather than the status quo. Regan also did not love the feeling of being undervalued and underpaid.

Red didn't think about such matters. He may as well have had no first or last name as part of his legend because everyone knew him as Red owing to his long red hair and beard. He could have been an extra in a movie about raping and pillaging Vikings! Red the Viking!

Red stopped the van somewhere outside Birkenhead. Regan woke up, startled. He had one of those Where the fuck am I? Who the fuck am I? moments, a mild panic until he recognized his surroundings and snapped into his faux identity. There was the familiar sinking feeling in the pit of his stomach in those moments. The feeling translated into a question in his head - Did I talk in my sleep? There was always a moment of panic, then relief as his secret was still safe. His sleeping lips had stayed immobile. Only he knew the answer to 'Who the fuck am I?'

The sight of Blue in the van also jolted him back to reality; that and the sound of Red's voice. They had met Blue about six months earlier . Blue was a part of the 'hippie scene' in mid-Wales where Regan and Red had established themselves to infiltrate an LSD drugs gang, a police investigation known as Operation Perfume. Both men were undercover for twelve months, a year of 'living a lie' as infiltrators. The first few months had been spent living in the van. It was an old Ford Transit with faded, blistered, pale blue paint, its panels decorated with many scratches and streaks of surface rust. But it had been home for the two undercover cops, evidenced by the mattresses, sleeping bags and detritus that had gathered over time in the back of the van.

"Steve, shift yer arse. It's your turn to drive. We'll be at the Mersey Tunnel in a few minutes," rang out the unmistakable West Country tones of Red.

That was the arrangement. Regan knew Liverpool and reckoned he could find the hotel in Mount Pleasant, where Blue had arranged to meet his Canadian friend, Bill. The two undercover cops had agreed to drive Blue to Liverpool to meet the Canadian. Blue had said enough to whet their appetite. Bill sounded like a 'player' in the drugs world.

The hotel had seen better days. The disinterested receptionist told all three men to go to Room 207. Bill let them into the room. Blue and Bill chatted and caught up on old times. Regan and his partner drank the whiskey that Bill poured, and listened. An hour passed before Bill wanted a change of scenery .

"Pint of Guinness for me," Regan said, as all four men walked into the American Bar in Lime Street. Blue went to the bar and ordered the drinks. In fact, he had bought most of the drinks on the way to Liverpool from Wales as his way of saying thanks for the ride. But on this occasion Bill handed him a fistful of £20 notes before Blue left the table. They settled into a dark corner of the bar, seated at a dirty greasy table that had seen gallons of beer spills in its lifetime. The beer mats stuck to the veneered top. They made a 'glooping' sound as Regan tried to reposition one.

"These are the two guys I was telling you about," Blue said.

Bill sort of grunted. They carried on sitting at the dirty table, Blue now doing most of the talking. Regan weighed Bill up, taking a good look at his face and the eyes in particular. Cold grey eyes like a dead fish. But they were fisheyes set in a bloated face. Regan could not see any glint, soul, or expression in them. Just dead. On occasions Bill would turn his gaze in turn to either Red or Regan. Sinister, Regan thought and believed he was a serious 'player.'

The chat, mainly by Blue, carried on for about an hour. During that time the cops learned that Bill, although a Canadian, spent most of his time in Miami, Florida. Bill also confirmed that he had been searching for a fast motorboat. The search had taken him not only to the Isle of Man but also to Panama and the South of France. Regan drank his beer throughout. Time flew, and he started to think ahead about where they could carry on drinking. It was getting towards that time when it would be too late to wander into a pub unless you were in the know and could find a 'lock-in.'

Regan had been away from Liverpool for too long to have that intimate knowledge. And besides, he would not want to risk his cover by walking into a boozer he knew well. More to the point, where the clientele knew him, the real 'him', well. The pub idea faded. They decided to eat, and Regan knew an Indian restaurant in nearby Bold Street.

The drinking and conversation carried on throughout the curry meal. Bill had now regained the lead role in the talking stakes. He was telling Blue how much he needed to find a fast eighty-foot boat. Bill spoke to the undercover cops directly for the first time.

"Listen I've got an operation going over in BC involving snow, not any old shit, got my markets, nothing over here. Coke is pure, straight from Bolivia. Retails at $24,000 a pound. If you guys are into that sort of bread, then I may be your man. What do you say to that?"

Blue pushed back his Stetson and said, "Listen, Bill, these two guys are my friends, now we're out for the night let's not talk about this."

"Excuse me, excuse me, Blue, Blue, Blue - let the guys think about it and sleep on it."

There was no more conversation about cocaine in the restaurant. But they spoke with a friendly waiter. He gave them a quick guide to clubs to go to, hookers and prices and he mentioned the

She Club. Regan knew it and they decided to go there. The waiter arranged for a taxi to take them. The only problem Regan foresaw was getting past security, as it was late. They weren't members nor did a member accompany them to sign in at the door. Also, they had to factor in that Red, Blue and Regan, looked like members of a rock band. Some may have said they all looked like hippies with their long hair, beards and denims. Similar but different - Red with his wild red hair and ginger beard, Blue wearing his Stetson, and Regan's tall lean build, wearing his favourite Aviators even at night.

But there are always 'ways and means'. Regan did the talking as he had the local dialect, a dialect distinctive throughout Britain, an accent difficult to understand to the first-time listener. In his pre-undercover days, a sight of a warrant card would have guaranteed entry. But that was the old Steve - he had kept his real first name. His pleas did not impress the security gorillas. But then he glimpsed a fist reaching across towards the chief gorilla. The fist belonged to Bill. It contained at least three £20 notes, maybe a week's wages for these guys. No one spoke another word. In place of words there was a sweeping gesture by the chief gorilla pointing towards the entrance.

Once inside, two things happened Regan would never forget. He started dancing but kicked off his shoes on the wooden dance floor. He had always wanted to dance bare-footed and now granted himself that wish! It helped that he was now inebriated. He had no sooner got on the dance floor and started to sway solo to the rhythms when he saw a good looking, vivacious young woman. She was a brunette, slim and wearing a pencil skirt showing off her hips and legs. She joined him on the dance floor and smiled.

She laughed a lot. He liked that. He liked her. She reminded him of a woman he once knew – his deceased wife. The brunette's constant glances at his feet made him feel a little uncomfortable; he believed he had the ugliest feet in the world. But she simply said, "I have always wanted to dance with a guy who kicks off his shoes and dances barefoot." He liked her even more.

They danced for a while, and when the slow stuff came on, got cheek to cheek. She smelled good, too. He could feel her hips push into his groin and his 'other brain' reacted, pushing hard against his denim jeans. She liked that. She started to thrust and grind her hips to the beat of the music, a slow and sensuous rhythm. He found out she was a nurse at a local hospital and clubbing with her friend, also a nurse, on their night off. She had all night free and threw in for good measure that she wasn't in any rush in the morning either! Regan could not believe his luck.

Chapter 3

LATER, REGAN AND THE sexy nurse made their way over to the table where Red, Blue and Bill were sitting, drinking and talking. Regan's new friend called out to her co-worker to join them. They now had a six-some! The girls went to the bathroom to powder their noses. The four guys started to chat. This is when the second unforgettable thing happened.

While Regan had been dancing, Red, Blue and Bill had clearly gotten around to talking business, drug smuggling. Red later told Regan the gist of the conversation that took place while he got busy on the dance floor.

Bill said to Red, "You guys are into a bit of business with shit, right? You'll have to think about what I said."

"Sounds a bit heavy to me," Red replied.

"You must have a man somewhere."

Red responded, "It's no good me saying yes or no until I've seen him though, is it?"

"Sure, Ginger, we're talking about a lot of bread now and in the future. Talking of bread, do you know anyone who will handle jewellery?"

"Warm?"

"Hot."

"Not really my area," came Red's reply.

Bill carried on, telling Red about a con trick to make $100 a day through his version of ringing the changes. Then he reverted to the topic of cocaine. Telling how he paid couriers $500 a trip, evading customs and using fast boats. Red listened and made a mental note of it all. There was also talk about legitimate businesses based in places like Nassau, Barbados, Antigua, Argentina, Panama, Miami, Georgetown Guyana and Vancouver Island.

Regan missed all this because he had been getting 'hot' on the dance floor. But no sooner had the girls left to go to the toilet, Red announced, "Ask him. I'm sure he will be okay with it." He nodded towards Regan, his partner.

Regan thought, but dare not say, what the fuck is he on about!

Blue spoke up, "Bill wants to know if you two can organize bringing a few keys of snow into Europe from Miami."

Fuck me! Regan thought but managed to keep a poker face.

The girls were away for about thirty minutes, so this next conversation happened over ten minutes, more or less.

"Yeah. It can be done," Regan said.

He paused then added, "Obviously depends on a few things but yeah, it's a go'er."

Bill had been quiet since Regan arrived back at the table. It made Regan jump a little when he spoke. Bill broke out from his taciturn shell by drawling on about how he was 'connected.' And how he was talking to the top echelon of the 'Cartel.' Of course, Regan knew he was referring to the drug gangs of South America. They were some of the most notorious and violent drug cartels in existence. Regan started to feel a little nervous at this point. His earlier 'lower regions excitement' now subsided; an 'excitement' provoked by his newfound female companion. She had become secondary.

Bill ceased talking just like he started. No warning. No intros and no endings. One minute there were words and then nothing.

It unsettled Regan. Total silence took over the whole table. Regan knew few people can deal with silence that goes on for longer than a few seconds. It feels uncomfortable. Many stupid people feel an urgent need to fill the verbal vacuum. Often with crap. Regan knew this was not an occasion to become a stupid person.

All kinds of thoughts started to rush around his head. Regan thought,

What if this? What if that?

Regan had often maintained no one can train cops about such situations or teach them how to react. He knew it's not possible to go to undercover class to learn how to cope. He also knew calmness is inbuilt. Regan believed you either have it or you don't. It's that simple. Perhaps the silence lasted for about one minute. Or longer?

During the whole time Bill and Regan stared at each other. Not in any kind of confrontational way – just staring. Holding eye contact between the two of them. Bill's cold grey eyes gave nothing away. Regan thought he had the eyes of a killer. He could be a killer. He's a gangster - part of the mob. At that point Bill's mouth moved again, no warning, not even a clearing of the throat.

"Are you guys cops?"

Wham! Fuck! Regan thought. The question rattled around inside Regan's brain. He knew it was often asked when undercover. Regan knew the first time was the worst. The mind raced, Has my cover been blown? Am I a fucking useless undercover cop? Do I look, smell and talk like a cop?

Regan also knew it was a test. He decided to react with aggression, "You fucking what? Yeah, course I am, and you're the fucking Pope!"

Bill laughed with his facial muscles but not with those fisheyes.

That took Regan by surprise. He didn't think humour was part of the Canadian's repertoire.

Then Bill's killer looks returned.

"If you guys are, then…"

The Canadian raised one hand next to Regan's head. Then he joined his forefinger and middle finger in the shape of a gun and pointed them at Regan. The 'gun' rested on his head so that Regan could feel the tips of Bill's fingers against his skin.

What followed was a simulated assassination. A 'double-tap' from a silenced semi-automatic pistol favoured by professional hitmen the world over. A close-range execution.

Regan went cold when he saw the Canadian mouth the silenced spitting sound. Twice, as two imaginary shells splattered his brains out of the gaping exit wounds at the far side of his head. This was personal.

Pop! Pop!

Regan jumped up from his seat, pushing Bill's hand away. Bill rose too, but Regan's push unbalanced Bill making him stumble on the chair leg. As Bill staggered backwards, he reached down for the gun in the ankle holster. Regan knew it and clenched his fist ready to strike. He was ready to kick Bill's hand, too. He was ready to do whatever it took.

By sheer serendipity the girls returned to the table. They had seen nothing. Regan and Bill sat down. The conversation switched to the humdrum. They had another couple of drinks each and the mood was convivial. All six left the She Club about 2 am and a taxi driver dropped them at a deserted illegal drinking den. They carried on drinking until about 6 am. The place served food too, so the night was finished off by all six eating a meal. The mood remained cordial throughout.

Regan's newfound female companion returned to the hotel with him and stayed. They did not sleep until about 7:30 in the morning as they took plenty of time in getting to know each other well. Regan woke up about 11 am the same day and found his bed empty. She had gone. He showered and looked in the mirror as his back felt painful. She had left her mark – literally, scratches running down both sides of his back from shoulders to waist.

Two unforgettable things in one night! Perhaps three? Regan thought I also danced barefooted!

All four guys left the hotel in Liverpool and drove back to Wales in the van.

Chapter 4

LIVERPOOL TO WALES, September 1976

REGAN COULD FEEL HIS head pounding, body dehydrated. He blamed himself, too much to drink. He forced himself to concentrate. His life, and that of Red's, may depend on him. The stakes rose during this drive back to Wales. One thought would not leave Regan – should he go rogue? It flashed through his mind like a car blinker. But he couldn't turn it off. The thought of riches from this connection to the Bolivian and Miami cocaine trade wouldn't leave him. Images of blondes and Jaguars ran through his head like a constant slideshow. Other images played but he forced them from his mind, images of loved ones past and present. Regan concentrated on the pleasant images. They agreed with him and stirred his inner self save for one image. It was a mental picture of his sick mother.

It is a long drive from Liverpool to mid-Wales. Wales is a small country and has a long coastline. There are mountains between the coast and the Welsh border with England. Those mountains prevent easy road access to anywhere in the middle of Wales. The four of them crammed into the van for the arduous journey. 'Shoulder to shoulder' was an understatement.

This was going to be a trip lasting several hours in the company of a gangster, Bill, and two major drug dealers in the Canadian and

Blue. Yet, Regan's main concern was the hangover. Despite the jaded feelings in body and mind Regan knuckled down and concentrated.

Those hours in the van and the occasional pit stop gave Bill ample opportunity to talk or shut up. He talked, and if anything, his tone was more serious than the previous night.

With a face set in stone, Bill said, "Guys, this is serious shit. I need a new market and this country is it. You have all these rock bands. All those guys are serious coke heads. They need quality powder and I am Mister Quality. I need good people like you two and Blue to set up the British connection."

Red concentrated on driving. Regan nodded along in tune with Bill's plan but did not speak.

Blue broke the silence, "No problem."

Another silence.

Blue added, "The south of France too."

"Excuse me!" Bill went red in the face and puffed out his already bloated cheeks.

"Bill, it's the jet set scene there. Millionaires, big yachts - the whole scene. Like a French Miami. We gotta get our cocaine into there, too."

Bill punched the faded roof lining.

"Fuck me! You nearly made me crash," shouted Red.

Bill raised his voice at Blue, "No way! You don't take on more than one place at a time. If you get caught you only get caught in one place, not three or four! What have I told you before? You are not listening!" Bill, the teacher and Blue the student.

Bill's outburst spelled out an abrupt end to the discussion about a new market in the south of France. Bill calmed down and started talking again about ten minutes later. Those ten minutes were uncomfortable. Bill had reinforced Regan's thoughts of him being capable of killing.

"I got the source. No one ever forget that. Without me and Bolivia there is no coke. I can put my hands on 50-pound weight immediately. Today. One phone call.

"I'm talking $24,000 for one pound. I need to know if you guys can do it." He carried on outlining the plan.

"A pressed pound weight is no bigger than the average size wallet. It's easier to ship that way. Less chance of detection. It's easily hidden. What I need to know is, can you guys do it?"

But he was in full flow now. He did not pause for an answer.

"These are some of the basic rules. No rip offs, period. Your cut is what you sell it for. My advice is don't sell less than half weights. That way you're not getting close to the street punks. You start at twenty-four for one shipment of one weight. Three weights twenty-three. Five or more twenty-one, maybe twenty. Okay?"

"Okay." Regan nodded comprehensively as if this was an everyday occurrence.

"If you don't have that kind of bread, find someone who has. But tell him the price per pound and discount for quantity ...

"... This is pure snow when it leaves me, you can cut it and cut it and cut it. When you buy off me it's not like buying the shit off the street. Oh, and payment always in greenbacks."

There was no shutting Bill up. He was on a high. A high caused by his love of money and a big score.

They stopped to stretch cramped legs, take a leak and a gulp of fresh air. The pit stop was at a roadside pub. The hangover was still hanging over Regan. He gulped down three swift pints of beer mixed with lemonade. Ah! He felt better.

This was as good as it gets in undercover work. They were now the dealers – 'the man.' The strange thing was that Regan did not feel excited. That was a good thing. He knew it doesn't pay to show inner feelings when undercover. Besides, he did not feel like a cop. He was now Steve Regan, a wild, irresponsible man prepared to transgress if it produced results. The lack of excitement came naturally to him. A police supervisor's report once recorded that if he was any more laid back, he would be horizontal! Red was equally as cool. He acted with total indifference to events during the pit stop break.

Bill with his killer eyes set in a piggy face, Blue with Stetson, Red and Regan climbed back into the van. The plan was to drop off Blue and Bill near Lampeter so they could collect a rental car. Blue knew a farmer who rented out cars for hire. Before setting off again, Bill asked Blue how much he needed for the rental.

"About £20, I guess," Blue responded.

Bill reached down to the floor of the van and lifted his expensive looking leather attaché case to his lap. He fiddled with the combination lock until the clasps clicked open. Regan looked inside in astonishment. He saw bundles of £20 notes about one-inch-high fastened with a rubber band, about ten identical bundles. It must have totalled somewhere in the region of £10,000. That was a lot of bread! Something else caught his attention. It lay at the bottom of the case under some documents and folded shirts. It was the unmistakable blue grey colour of a protruding pistol barrel. Regan's stomach churned as he thought about last night's performance with the death threat.

The rest of the journey mainly consisted of Bill talking. Red and Regan listened and carefully made a mental note. Those mental notes ended up as a narrative in their report to Rick Green, the boss of Operation Perfume.

Bill explained the background to his operation. It was a one-man gig in Bolivia but helped out by two buddies. He always dealt with the same man in Bolivia and spoke with him directly. The Bolivian was not the cocoa leaf farmer. He bought the leaf and cooked it so it ended up as 100% cocaine product. That was what Bill was buying. He used five couriers to bring the product into the States and Canada. One, a former air hostess. Customs in Montreal knew her well, waved her through with a smile and a perfunctory "Hi Dawn." Bill used a bank in the Cayman Islands to launder his drugs cash and reckoned his profits were $64,000 per month.

He also sold himself as a promoter or fixer. A man with connections, boasting that with two phone calls he turned over one deal involving heroin worth $1,000,000 in the States. He never saw or went near the smack. Bill trusted Red and Regan. He started to push hard to find a money backer.

"There is no rush. I'll be around for the next two weeks," Bill drawled.

"You can get hold of me through Blue or the number I gave you," he added.

During the journey Bill had written down a Bristol address and telephone number. He gave it to Red as his contact details while in the UK. Not content with a huge plot to import coke into Britain, Bill revisited the issue of dealing in stolen jewellery. But, this time he extended his unlawful activities into diamond smuggling and porn. He was keen to extend his theatre of operations by recruiting the two undercover cops.

Chapter 5

SEPTEMBER 1976

REGAN SIGHED WITH RELIEF when the van reached the farm. It had been a long day. Regan was now ready to say their farewells to Bill before they set off for Bristol. That pleasant English city was to be an overnight stop for them prior to scouring the south coast marinas for a fast motorboat. Bill wanted to stay at the Holiday Inn. Regan guessed it was because it would be a welcome change from the seedy Liverpool hotel. Plus, a well-travelled Canadian would know what to expect from a Holiday Inn whether located in Bristol, Boston, Bangkok or Bolivia.

Regan's tall frame shuddered when Bill announced they would follow the van to Bristol. They had earlier told them that was their planned destination after arriving back in Wales. That was looking like a mistake. It concerned Regan. Before the van and the rental car set off, Bill spoke to both men, "Remember you know how to get hold of me, either through that number or Blue."

Red, nodding, said, "It may take longer than two weeks."

"When you are good and ready," came Bill's cool reply.

Bill walked over to Regan's side of the van. As he approached, he stressed they must find 'the man' and as quickly as possible. Regan assured him they would talk to the right people. Bill wanted a swift yes or no.

The van led the way. After all, it was a route Red and Regan knew blindfolded. In hushed tones and sign language, Red and Regan agreed not to discuss anything in the van. There could be a bug in here, was their collective thought. They were paranoid!

The M32 is a short spur of a motorway that leaves the M4 Wales to London motorway, connecting Bristol City Centre with the M4. At the Bristol end of the M32 the motorway changes into a regular main road. Red pulled over in a layby and the rental car containing Bill and Blue pulled in behind.

Red gave them directions to the Holiday Inn, Bristol and much to their relief Bill and Blue drove off toward the city centre. The normal route to Red's home in the Bristol suburbs would have taken about ten minutes. Red drove for the next forty-five minutes all over Bristol. The van turned into a dead-end road to check if they were followed and Red adopted every single counter-surveillance tactic he could think of. Finally, content they were not being followed, both cops exhaled a simultaneous sigh of relief and the same exclamation, "Fuck me!"

This warranted a special journey into the office to brief Rick Green and make a full record of the whole episode. They did just that the next day, the report fulsome and exact. They had also gathered that Bill had a Canadian passport, a British wife and two kids resident in the Isle of Man. It was believed his net worth was about $3,000,000 despite some Canadian tax problems. But Bill did say he wasn't sure about the exact amount as "he hadn't counted it lately!"

The night before seeing Rick Green, Regan had driven to his one bedroom flat an hour's drive from Bristol. Sleep came easy to

Regan. It had been an exhausting two days in the company of Bill and Blue, requiring full-on concentration to avoid any chance of a slip-up. Regan had nodded off. But he had one of those muscular spasms that jerk you out of your sleep. His thoughts turned to Bill and the events in Liverpool and the way back to Wales. He had a sixth sense something did not stack up. Something else bothered him. He could not shift the thoughts from his mind – Shall I go rogue? Can I go rogue?

Chapter 6

AUGUST 1976

HER MAJESTY'S CUSTOMS and Excise, known to many as simply Customs, is an arm of the United Kingdom's government responsible for ensuring taxes and duties payable are collected. Its remit is wide and powers draconian. It has many types of specialist investigators. Among other things, Customs is responsible for preventing and detecting the illegal import and export of controlled drugs, the investigation of organisations and individuals engaged in international drug smuggling, their prosecution and identification of the proceeds of such crime. It's fair to say there is a blurring of jurisdictional responsibilities between it and the police when it comes to drug trafficking. The relationship between the two has often been marked by in-fighting. Customs also employs undercover agents.

The telephone could be heard ringing some fifty yards distant through the empty corridors. An agent picked up and answered the call in a breathless voice.

"Yeah, Bill here."

"Good. I have been trying to get hold of you for two days now."

"Right. Is there something you want?"

"No. It's a new assignment for you."

"You're kidding. I just got back from Miami and was hoping to have a few days with Caroline. Can't it wait?"

"I hear you. Come and see me tomorrow, but I need you to start next week. You aren't travelling too far this time, Wales."

The phone clicked dead. Bill spoke to himself, "Wales?" He thought, At least it's August so I won't bloody freeze to death.

Bill Morris strode through the corridors in Tintagel House until he reached the offices occupied by Customs. It was at that point he showed his official identification to an armed guard. Tintagel House is a concrete, steel and glass edifice scarring the banks of the River Thames. It was home to secretive departments belonging to both London's Metropolitan Police and Customs. The same building, but offices separated by mutual distrust, loathing and armed guards.

Five minutes later Bill was seated in front of his boss, Dennis Marks.

"Nice suit, Bill. Milan?"

"Nope. I bought it in Hong Kong last year."

"Good job you told me that. If it was Milan, I would have had you investigated." No humour accompanied those words.

Bill did not react. He knew it did come from Milan and cost over £1000 but why tell. He had splurged during a shopping trip to Milan with Caroline. She and Bill were an item. In any case, Caroline Sewell could have afforded to buy it herself if she so wished. She was a successful criminal barrister with a thriving practice in London and had eyes on becoming Queen's Counsel and a judge.

They were an odd couple to a degree. Bill was thirty-three years old, divorced, with two kids living with their mother on the Isle of Man where his ex-father in law owned a private bank. Bill was rough and ready and had married into a family with money and class. He had looks that did not stand out in a crowd. Bill was an ordinary looking guy with a chubby face and a squashed nose that threatened to spread from one side of his mouth to the other. His appearance would have been at home in a boxing ring.

Bill considered Caroline Sewell to be his new girlfriend. Caroline was from a moneyed family, old money. She had attended the finest schools in England and graduated with a First Class Honours Degree in politics, philosophy and economics from the LSE. Caroline, at thirty-nine, had lost none of her good looks. Sometimes, she could effortlessly pass for a thirty-year-old woman. She did like danger. She liked Bill because of what he did and the stories he told her. She also preferred younger men.

The two had met when she prosecuted a drug trafficking gang. It was a showpiece trial at the Old Bailey that lasted three months. Bill had been a Customs liaison officer in the case and they got to know each other. He became a frequent visitor to her luxurious Chelsea flat with a view down the River Thames towards Westminster.

The suit was one of the few extravagant items he had bought. It did not make for good practice to be too flash. He did not have the formal education of Caroline but he knew about life. He was savvy. His thoughts wandered to Caroline because his boss was boring the shit out of him. I wonder what she is doing right now, Bill thought.

Chapter 7

SAME MONTH - AUGUST 1976

CAROLINE SEWELL PUSHED her way aboard the crowded Tube train before the doors closed. It was hot in there and full of perspiring bodies, some of whom enjoyed the close proximity to her female shape a little too much. It was a common experience for her and many other attractive women to feel a male groin thrust in to her shapely backside. Over the years she had developed a reflex response – a sharp blow from her elbow to the sleazeball's ribs. Thank God I only have a few stops, she thought.

Miss Sewell, as she was known to her clerks in her chambers, and similarly addressed by judges in the courtroom, had delivered her jury speech the previous afternoon. Caroline could now relax. Nothing to do the next day except to listen to the judge's summing up and wait for the jury's verdict.

After leaving the Inner London Sessions courthouse close to the Elephant and Castle, she had spent the entire evening in a Fleet Street wine bar with colleagues. The Criminal Bar of England and Wales, especially in London, is as prone to gossip as many other walks of life, if not more so. As the evening drew to a close, she became the centre of gossip. Some may have called it speculation. It was the time in the legal calendar when new Queen's Counsel were announced. Although many of her colleagues deemed her to be a racing certainty to be on the list, Caroline could only dream. It was the penultimate step to her ambition – becoming a Circuit Judge. She believed she would look good in that red sash. But what really attracted her was the pension.

She was ruthless and didn't care much about colleagues or friends. All she cared about was her career. It had been like that since she graduated from the London School of Economics, right through Bar School and honed through all her days practising law. She was bright, sassy, attractive with a line in humour that was ... well, non-existent. Caroline saw everything and everybody as black and white. There were no shades of grey. She had realised at an early stage that remaining a barrister, even a silk, was not for her. As a barrister, she was essentially an independent contractor. A self-employed practitioner who would have to fund her own future in the shape of a pension. She had learned from Daddy the importance of a pension in her old age. Although circuit judges were not paid excessive sums of money, the pay was more than adequate. It was at retirement age she found the income to be at its most attractive, owing to a judicial pension.

Caroline soon established a steady practice within a few years of qualifying as a barrister. After ten years she was earning a high-end five figure salary. Like many at the Criminal Bar, she both prosecuted and acted as defence counsel. Of the two, she preferred to prosecute and knew it would help in her ambitions. A pleasant flat in Chelsea overlooking the River Thames soon became affordable. That is where she now lived, to all intents and purposes alone, except when she had invited male guests. They sometimes stayed one night, sometimes more and occasionally for a whole week. Part of that depended on how good they were in bed. Caroline liked strong men. She liked rough sex. If a man passed the audition, he may stay more than one night. Caroline liked a change. She didn't want steady until she met Bill Morris. He also passed the audition in spite of his porcine looks Caroline often fantasied about rape in her sexual liaisons. Bill was so good at that she thought sometimes he was raping her before reminding herself it was merely role playing between two consenting adults.

But steady was not an option with Bill. She had met him through his work with Customs and knew he was frequently away from London, sometimes abroad, for long stretches of time. There was something about Bill that attracted her like no other man she had met. He was as ruthless as she was. Bill also had connections. Those connections came as a surprise to her but she welcomed the surprise.

Running up the solid stone stairs of the old Inner London Sessions courthouse, Caroline heard her name called. Turning around, she saw her old friend Suzie . They had been at Bar School at Gray's Inn together and shared many a secret from those heady days of hard study and even harder partying.

"Hi, Suzie!"

"Caroline, do you have a moment?"

"Sure, what gives?"

"Got any powder?"

Caroline looked beyond her colleague, checking if anyone was in earshot. She turned her head and repeated the process for what or who lay behind her. Caroline grabbed Suzie's shoulders and shook her.

"Never, never talk about that to me in public. Got it?"

Suzie's ashen face changed to puce. "Yeah. Sorry. Just so hung over and I need a buzz to do my jury speech."

Grabbing her hand roughly, Caroline pulled Suzie into an empty room normally reserved for barristers to interview their clients. The door slammed shut behind them. Inside, Caroline spoke in hushed tones. Hushed but fierce at the same time. Her eyes bore into Suzie's skull.

"Listen to me and listen good. You are two weeks into a month's product and you are asking me for more! What the fuck, Suzie!"

"Sorry, Cee," she replied as her eyes moistened.

"Don't start fucking crying on me. Pull yourself together, woman."

Suzie wiped away the teardrops. "I'm just so stressed, Cee. Using more than I usually do. You know what it's like."

"Well, no, I don't, actually. For once only you can have some. Follow me."

Like a dutiful puppy, Suzie followed Caroline to the WC used by female barristers next to the female only robing room. Caroline didn't care if they were disturbed. She had already planned to embrace and kiss Suzie in the event they were surprised. Caroline produced a small plastic sachet and tipped half the white powder content on top of the low-level WC flush. She then chopped it with a safety razor she also kept in her purse, arranging it into two straight lines. Suzie had rolled a five-pound note into a cylindrical shape. The two barristers each snorted one line of cocaine with relish. Caroline Sewell threw back her blonde hair and Suzie did the same with her long auburn hair, like an alcoholic throws back the head siphoning whiskey dregs from a near empty glass.

"Thanks, Cee."

"Don't ask again. You will have to wait to next month for some more. Usual or do you want more?"

"Better double it up."

"Okay. Same routine, same money, but double."

"Yeah, no worries."

Caroline was certain of her supply chain. That was the surprise of Bill's connections.

Suzie and Caroline entered the female robing room separately to don their court attire, including the horsehair wig and barrister's gown. Next stop for both was a coffee in the barristers' dining area then to their respective courtrooms. They sat sipping their coffees with Callum Colhoun, a Scottish barrister. Callum and Caroline knew each other well. They had plenty in common.

All three barristers finished the coffee and went to their respective court rooms. Suzie delivered a rousing jury speech. No one suspected it was inspired by drugs. Caroline sat quietly as the judge in her case summed up the case both for and against the accused for the benefit of the jury. His Honour Judge Pinderford finally gave the jury directions to the relevant law. The jury then retired to consider its verdict.

The last jury member had left the courtroom when Judge Pinderford said, "Miss Sewell."

Caroline rose to her feet, at the same time replying, "Your Honour?"

"I suppose congratulations are in order."

"Sorry, Your Honour, I have no idea why."

"Permit me to be the first then. You will be taking Silk."

"Your Honour, I am ...." Caroline spluttered and was, for once in her life, at a loss for words.

The walk back to the robing room seemed to take an age. Caroline was deep in thought. The leaked news of her impending elevation to the ranks of Queen's Counsel, taking silk, was the next step to her ultimate goal – a judgeship. It was now imperative she kept the lid on her extra-curricular activities. Even better, she mused, time to offload them as a part of history, her personal history – baggage she would not wish anyone to discover. Who could she trust? she thought. The answer came to her in a flash. She had earlier been drinking coffee in his company in the barristers' dining room.

Caroline Sewell looked and talked the part of a London barrister. For work, she dressed in the uniform black skirt, black jacket and black court shoes. The white blouse was part of the barrister look. Her long blonde hair tied back with a black ribbon gave her a somewhat severe look but was still attractive. She had clawed her way up through the thousands of hopefuls practising criminal law in London. Most were no real competition to her. They had their heads turned by the fanciful romantic notion that life at the Criminal Bar was exciting, just like those TV programmes. Caroline had soon discovered there was no romance, no excitement. It was a mixture of hard work and wearing out shoe leather travelling from one court to another.

It was the tiring nature of the profession that first led to Caroline using cocaine. It made her feel good. The problem was that she liked it too much. It was addictive and expensive. Like most problems she encountered, Caroline found an answer. She started dealing in coke to other barristers also in need of a regular toot. Initially, it was to a select few in London. It had grown to a network of fifty and upwards throughout London, Birmingham and Manchester. She was known as 'Lady C.' Like Topsy, it had grown. Her driving thought now was how to end her cartel before it destroyed her ambition.

Caroline Sewell picked up the phone once she got home. She dialled and waited for someone to pick up. "Callum, it's me, Cee.

Just be a good boy and do as you are told. Don't ask me any questions over the phone. Understood?"

Callum said, "Of course, darling."

"Okay, come to my place at 3 pm Saturday."

Callum Colhoun was a London barrister with a fierce cocaine habit. He spent most of his time defending out on circuit – in the provinces – involving weeks at a time on lengthy trials away from home. Those weeks were spent in hotels, a lonely existence. Callum whiled away the leisure hours entertaining local prostitutes in the seclusion of his hotel room. They were content with the price he paid for sexual services and the copious amounts of coke he shared with them. In turn, he was content, as this way he could forget his stint in the court room defending murderers and rapists .

Caroline trusted him. He was one of her oldest customers. She spelled out the finality of her proposal to Callum. Opening the wall safe in her Chelsea flat, Caroline handed him a small black book. He now had the telephone number of a man called Dash, one of her dealers, and all her regular customers. She had two dealers. The book did not contain the name or number of the second dealer. Those details were imprinted on her memory. She knew him well. It was Bill.

"The business is yours. I just demand one thing. Never, never breathe a word to anyone about me. It's as simple as that. Do you understand?"

Callum nodded.

"I can't hear you," she spat.

He said, "I hear you, loud and clear."

"Needless to say, this meeting never happened."

"What meeting?"

Caroline moved over to Cullum and gave him an air kiss, "Mwahhhh!"

Callum thought, Bitch! He had never liked her. He only tolerated her because she was the source of his regular supply of cocaine.

Once her colleague had left, she made a phone call from the safety of her flat. It was to the dealer she had 'given' to Callum. Caroline had noted it before giving away the black book. The dealer was now aware that Callum was "the man" and she had retired.

Caroline found the corkscrew in the open kitchen and thrust it into the virgin cork of a bottle of fine claret. Time to relax, she thought. But first she went back into the wall safe and removed her own personal stash. This was ninety-five percent pure Colombian sourced from someone neither Callum, nor anyone else would ever know about, Bill.

Part of the white powder was released onto the ebony table in the living room. Chop, chop, chop - she arranged it into two similar white lines, took out her tube kept for these occasions and snorted both lines of powder.

Boom! went her brain. God that feels good, she thought.

Chapter 8

SHEFFIELD – AUGUST, 1976

CALLUM COLHOUN WAS in Sheffield and up to his usual tricks. He was a pugnacious advocate in court. His abrasive style earned him enemies amongst both judges and barrister colleagues. Callum did not care. He liked sailing close to the wind and seeing what he could get away with. His motto may have been – 'Rules are there to be broken.'

Those rules were many. He had been practising at the Criminal Bar of England and Wales for fifteen years. Now aged forty, he was often instructed as counsel in serious cases such as murder. Callum had developed a niche acting as leading junior counsel whereby he was assisted by a second junior counsel in serious cases. He was an expert in manipulating the legal aid gravy train to maximise his earnings.

Callum was in the middle of a murder trial in Sheffield, a trial expected to last ten weeks. His only problem was he was also instructed to appear simultaneously in another trial in London. The logistics involved would have forced most to choose between one trial or the other, not Callum. He had his second junior cover for him so he could pocket two lucrative sets of fees. A ploy that came unstuck when the two trial judges were dining in their Inn and one casually mentioned the upstart Colhoun. Their sharp legal minds did not take long to work out his deception. A brief letter from the Bar Council summoned Callum to explain himself. The summons was one more thing on Callum's mind. There was also a statutory demand from the Inland Revenue to deal with. He didn't worry about much but the tax demand gave him sleepless nights as he had not filed a tax return in fifteen years. Callum responded to these concerns by using more cocaine, drinking more alcohol and getting laid by more hookers.

"How is Lady C these days?" inquired Dash. He was the drug dealer Caroline had passed on to Callum.

"Good as always but never mind her. I have customers waiting. Where is my order for the half kilo?"

"Man, don't be so impatient. You only ordered the product three days ago. I'll meet you in the usual place. Tuesday at 4 pm. Okay?"

"Right. Be there."

"I will... one thing... do you want a new girl? Pretty young Thai thing."

"Yeah. A change is as good as a rest. So yeah. Tell her to come to my room, ten tonight."

"Usual room? Same hotel?"

"Yes," Callum replied then replaced the handset on his phone in the Sheffield hotel room. This was his 'home from home.' He spent half of his working year there following his chosen line of work; defending killers and rapists as a fearless London barrister. Callum upset the local cosy arrangements between judiciary and local counsel, the latter always mindful of reputation. Callum wanted money, not the reputation.

Callum was content for Dash to deliver the cocaine the following week because he was under no pressure from barristers who had placed orders for the coke. He had enough for his personal use to last him until then, so all was good. He decided to stay in the hotel that evening and have dinner courtesy of room service while he worked on some witness statements preparing to cross-examine a prosecution witness the following day.

The chicken cordon bleu remained half-eaten on the table in the centre of Callum's hotel room. There were also several empty cans of strong lager. The bottle of malt whiskey was on the table but as yet intact. Callum glanced at his watch when he heard the faint knock on the door. It was exactly 10 pm. Dressed only in black boxer shorts and navy-blue tee, he opened the door to see Mai standing there, smiling.

"Dash sent me," Mai said.

Callum did not answer. He held out his hand to Mai and gently pulled her inside his room. Callum discovered Mai was nineteen years old and had arrived in the UK from Thailand last month, ostensibly to work in a restaurant. They talked for a while, drank whiskey together then snorted a few lines of cocaine.

Four Sheffield detectives hauled Callum from his hotel bed. They saw the battered face and body of Mai slumped on the hotel room's carpeted floor. The hotel staff had heard the screams at 4 am so called the police. They summoned an ambulance to tend to the severe facial injuries Callum had inflicted on his victim. They also handcuffed Callum and took him to the police station.

At 8 pm the same day the police released Callum on bail to return to the police station so they could gather medical evidence to substantiate Mai's allegations of rape and causing grievous bodily harm. They imposed a condition of his bail that he was to return to London and come nowhere near Sheffield until his next appointment with the Sheffield detectives. Callum Colhoun's problems were intensifying; tax problems; professional discipline problems; the prospect of many years imprisonment for raping and inflicting grievous bodily harm on a pretty Thai call girl. Dash was furious when he heard of it. He believed Callum Colhoun was totally out of control. He had gone too far this time.

Chapter 9

TINTAGEL HOUSE, LONDON, August 1976

BILL'S THOUGHTS ABOUT Caroline stopped and his concentration returned when Dennis Marks' phone rang. It was a short and sharp conversation and before his boss could replace the handset in the cradle Bill said, "You didn't ask me to come here to talk about my suit. What's all this about Wales?"

"You know about Operation Perfume?"

"Yes, it's the police looking at the source of all the acid, the LSD, the whole hippie-dippy festival thing. What's that got to do with us?"

"Green has two men deep undercover in Wales. They have been there some time and Green wants to know if they have gone rogue."

"Fuck! I hate these jobs. Can't you give it to someone else? Why can't a police rubber-heel squad do it?"

"No, not really. There is an agent I had in mind, codename Blue, but he's not ready to go solo. He hasn't got the experience, at least not with us. He's out in Wales shacked up with a woman. Besides, it's a favour to Green. He's terrified of the Met getting wind of what he's up to so turned to me."

"I hear you. Blue... is he one of those secret squirrel guys who used to be part of the Met's SDS infiltration mob?"

"Afraid so."

"Shit! I hate those guys and what they do. End up living with innocent women. Have kids with them and all to bolster a back story. It's crap."

"Ours is not to wonder why, Bill ..."

"Ours is but to do and die ... yeah, I know," Bill retorted with a shrug of his broad shoulders.

Bill looked at his boss. He knew it was pointless discussing things any further. When Dennis Marks affected the straight face look, you accepted whatever he was suggesting. Marks was a calm man with innards of steel. Besides, Bill prided himself on his ability to read people and situations. It was what he did. It was also convenient to placate his boss. It prevented Marks looking too closely at Bill's activities.

"Okay, Dennis. Get Blue to call me and we will crank it up."

"Good man. Thanks, Bill."

Bill Morris was not in a good mood. He did not relish the prospect of working with agent Blue, no matter what he was like. Bill found the Met's secret activities abominable, an affront to decency. Nevertheless, he was a professional and placed the call to Blue's department head. They met the following week.

Chapter 10

MEMBURY MOTORWAY SERVICE Area, August 1976

"SO WHAT YOU GOT IN mind, Bill?"

Blue was loud in every conceivable way. Bill wondered how on earth this man in front of him could have buried himself deep undercover for so long. His voice was loud and so were his clothes. Blue wore a faded leather Stetson with a blue feather tucked inside the hat band. He was a big guy but looked larger in the Afghan coat he wore. Then Bill saw the cowboy boots with three-inch heels making Blue even taller than his six feet two inches.

Blue spoke in a mid-Atlantic drawl turned up to high volume. It was as well this meeting took place in Bill's car. But it did not belong to Bill - it was a Customs pool car. A nondescript Ford saloon. There were no markings and no tell-tale add-ons. It was 'as-is' straight out of the Dagenham factory except for the discreet microphones located in the front and rear of the car. Every word would be recorded and sent via a secreted aerial direct to GCHQ in Cheltenham for decoding. This was hi-tech kit the police only dreamed about and was another source of animosity between Customs and police. The cops always viewed Customs as better funded by government. Cynics would not find that surprising. Revenue to any government takes precedence over crime.

The meeting took place in the car park of the Membury Services on the M4 Motorway between London and Bristol. Bill chose a secluded quiet area to park, on the far side of the huge car park. Blue's description had been given to Bill so the sudden appearance of a six-footer resplendent in a leather Stetson and beard flowing down to his chest held no surprises. Blue sat in the front passenger seat and turned towards Bill.

"You must be Bill. The code is Tuesday."

The loud voice was a surprise. Bill was told about this but was still surprised.

"For fuck's sake, do you have to fucking shout?"

"I'm not. Am I?" Blue was taken aback at Bill's directness.

Bill instantly disliked Blue but thought, Stay cool. I have to work with this chump.

Blue lowered the tone and mock-whispered, "Is this better?"

Bill's hand grasped Blue's throat and squeezed – hard.

"Tuesday is the correct password and that's why I'm not gonna kill you here and now. Now I'm telling you for the record (Bill nodded in the direction of the hidden microphone) – you do everything I tell you, understood?"

With that Bill released his captive's throat. Blue managed a hoarse, "capiche." There was now an understanding who was boss. Or so Bill thought.

Blue had other ideas such as, No one does that to me and gets away with it. Blue had a wild side to his personality. He decided to join the Metropolitan Police Service at nineteen. His reasoning was that if he didn't he would end up in jail. He had always loved a fight. Blue was unconventional in his ways for a copper. It was what attracted the interest of the bosses at the Special Demonstration Squad. In no time at all he was recruited and indoctrinated into that unit's way of 'doing business' – 'by any means necessary' was its motto. Blue infiltrated a racist group and led their violent protests in South London. He was not averse to beating up on his own colleagues in furtherance of his cover. It ingratiated himself with the others in the group. He spent most of his time with them and that is where he met his partner, Rachael. At first, she was a convenience, a part of his cover story. The longer they spent together, the more he liked her until they fell in love and had a child together.

"Okay, down to business. What do you know about Operation Perfume?"

"The acid thing? Right?"

"Yeah but what else do you know?"

"Nothing much except I heard there were big acid dealers near where I live and a rumour about an LSD factory making millions of microdots."

"Here's the thing. The police have two undercovers operating near you, called Regan and a guy known as Red."

"Yeah, I know them. In fact, I met them in the pub a few months back. They're good. I didn't know they were undercover."

"Right, that makes things even easier. I want you to pal up to them. Get them to meet me in Liverpool."

"Why Liverpool?"

"All part of the cover story and if you stop interrupting, I'll get round to the whole story."

"Okay," Blue purred in a mock whisper.

Bill smiled, "Better. Have you checked in yet?"

Blue nodded and said, "Yeah. We're in the Three Swans in Hungerford. I left Rachael and our baby there to come see you."

"Good to know you can follow instructions."

"Yeah boss. Yessir, Boss," mocked Blue in a deep American drawl.

BILL TURNED THE IGNITION key and drove off to the hotel. Blue showed him up to the room in the old coaching house hotel and knocked three times on the room door. Rachael opened it and let them in.

Bill was unable to take his eyes off her. He undressed her with his eyes and Rachael knew it. Rachael Owens was twenty-five years old, petite and five feet two inches tall. She had black hair tied up at the back and was wearing a floral-patterned dress that came to just above her knees, revealing well-shaped legs. Bill also noticed the outline of her small but pert breasts under the dress.

"Hi baby, this is Bill. Bill, Rachael," said Blue.

"Hi, honey," replied Bill. Rachael nodded in acknowledgment but didn't speak.

Bill tossed the car keys across to Blue who caught them. "Hey, Blue! Do me a favour. Go get a bottle of Four Roses, my favourite bourbon. The briefing will take a while and we may as well have something decent to drink."

Blue replied, "Not sure if they have that in Hungerford."

"That's what the car keys are for. Go to Marlborough or New-bury, anywhere, even Kentucky, as long as you find it," laughed Bill.

"Can't we just ..." Blue was cut off in mid-sentence.

"Blue, just do as you're told," grunted Bill.

Blue left the room, slamming the door behind him. Fucking arsehole! he thought.

The hotel room was small. There was little room around the double bed and on one side there was even less room. It was taken up with a cot. Fannie, Blue and Rachael's daughter was asleep.

"Hey Rach, what about a blow job?" Bill smirked. "No one will know except us two."

"One, my name is Rachael not Rach. Two, how can I put this delicately .... Go fuck yourself!"

Bill rose from the solitary chair in the room and grabbed Rachael's shoulders from behind. He didn't speak. He used one hand to lift up her dress and slid his hand all the way to her left breast. In seconds Rachael was spun about and now on her back on the bed. She looked at her baby and made a decision. Whatever happened she was not going to wake up her baby.

Rachael soon found out what was about to happen. She bit her lip until she felt the warm blood. It distracted her as Bill pulled up her dress, ripped off her panties, and pulled her towards him by the hips like a rag doll. He pulled again but this time so he could raise her legs upwards then pushed them outwards. Rachael's knees were apart but close to her head as Bill thrust deep inside her. She bit deeper into her own flesh. It took seconds for Bill to groan and deposit his seed inside her.

Bill's trousers were still down by his ankles as he sought the chair. He pulled them up, zipped and buckled his belt. He sat in the chair in silence, listening to his breath return to normal and his pulse to stop racing. What the fuck did I do that for? was Bill's only thought. No thoughts at all for Rachael. She raised herself from the bed, smoothed down her dress, and ran into the bathroom clutching her torn panties. Bill heard the shower running.

When Blue returned with a bottle of bourbon, he found Rachael sitting on the bed holding their baby. Bill was on the single chair watching BBC news on the TV. No one spoke except Blue. "I'll get glasses from the bathroom." Still no one spoke.

"Rachael, go take the baby for a walk. Bill and I need to talk."

Rachael looked at Blue in puzzlement tinged with fear but knew it was best not to say anything. Within seconds she had dressed the baby and picked up the folded stroller. Blue opened the door and they left.

The next hour was taken up with Bill giving Blue chapter and verse about the cover story and their goal – to see if Regan and Red had gone rogue.

Chapter 11

EARLY SEPTEMBER 1976

SOME WEEKS LATER BILL Morris checked in to the Feathers Hotel in Liverpool and was given the key to Room 207. One flight of stairs took you to the first floor and room 207 was down the corridor. Bill thought, What a dump. He also thought, Why 207? It should be 107. This isn't the States. Then he recalled the city's history built on sea trade with America. Once the home port of many fine ships, the docks were now home to museums and cafes. Must have done it to keep the Yanks happy, I guess, Bill mused and smiled at the irony. He also thought about his Canadian connections and how his mother had crossed the Atlantic in a Cunard liner sailing from Liverpool to New York. She planned a new life in America but Bill had been raised mainly in Canada. Morris was not his birth family name. It was a Sicilian name. His mother's maiden name was Di Maria. That was the name he was given at birth. He never knew his father.

A few days earlier Blue had left his stone cottage in rural mid-Wales after his goodbye to Rachael and his baby daughter Fannie. His daughter was the apple of his eye and often made him rue keeping Rachael in the dark about his true identity. It's the price I have to pay, was his means of justification. Although unmarried, Blue and Rachael were a team. She cooked for him, cleaned for him, doted on him and asked no questions.

Blue, no one except Rachael knew his name and even that wasn't his real name, was embedded in Wales originally by the Metropolitan Police SDS, Special Demonstrations Squad, and its predecessor the Special Operations Squad, targeting and infiltrating the Free Wales Army. Those individuals had fire-bombed many Welsh homes owned by English folks, usually as a second home away from London. They had links to the IRA and Basque terrorist groups and so were deemed worthy of infiltration by the Special Branch. The SDS was spawned by Special Branch. It was the dirty tricks department and did stuff Special Branch dare not do. The SDS was so secretive not even the Met Commissioner knew what it was up to. Its motto – 'By Any Means Necessary.'

Rachael never told Blue what had happened in the Hungerford hotel room. There was no need. Blue just knew. He swore to get even one day, by any means necessary!

REGAN AND RED WERE often to be found in a Tregaron pub in mid-Wales. It was there Blue reacquainted himself with the two Operation Perfume undercover cops.

Blue, as ever larger than life, boomed, "Hey, rascals! What you drinking?"

"Seeing it's you, a large Scotch. Oh, and a beer," laughed Regan.

"Okay, what about you, Red?"

"Pint of beer will be fine," Red smiled.

"Okay boys, you got it."

A heavy drinking session followed with a few games of pool and a number of joints. Blue could hold both his liquor and weed. Later in the session they were joined by Yosser. Everyone knew him as Yosser. The day wore on. Yosser suggested a game of cards back at his place. All agreed and the small band of hippies walked to Yosser's home, a small stone cottage decked out as some kind of Hindu shrine.

The cards were secondary to the booze, weed and laughter. The music lurked in the background but was never going to drown out the chat and laughter between these guys. Not one of them seemed to have a job. There was an implicit understanding they all wheeled and dealed in some product or another. No questions asked. This was mid-Wales where people came to escape the busy city, escape nosy neighbours and twitching curtains. This part of the United Kingdom promised the alternative lifestyle with a capital 'A.'

The card school broke up. Blue decided to stay with Regan and Red for the night in their rented cottage about three hundred yards away from Yosser's home. This was a cottage they rented as winter approached. Living in the van had become impractical. All three woke the next day with blinding headaches, the hangover from hell.

"Only one thing for it," Regan croaked through dry lips and arid throat, "hair of the dog."

"Fucking A," agreed Blue and Red followed suit.

Several pints of Guinness were the order of the day for breakfast, no food – just Guinness. "Guinness is food," cried Regan. "It was food for my father, his father and all my Paddy ancestors!"

Red frowned and said, "Begorrah, not the Irish bullshit again."

All three had toked some weed before the pub "breakfast." No doubt that contributed to all three howling with laughter at the last exchange between Red and Regan.

The thing was - from both perspectives, Blue on one side and Regan and Red on the other, a relationship had formed. All three felt comfortable in the company of each other. The next day Blue cashed in on this camaraderie when he asked Regan and Red to drive him to Liverpool to meet an old friend of his. The name of the friend was Bill.

There was a knock at the door of Room 207, the Feathers Hotel, Liverpool. Bill was half asleep but in a state of dress. By habit he reached under the pillow to feel for the handle of his gun. It was there and he slipped it into the ankle holster still strapped to his leg. He opened the door of Room 207 and saw Blue, Regan and Red in the doorway.

Chapter 12

LATE SEPTEMBER 1976

REGAN KNEW THE TIME was ripe to call Bill following the meeting in Liverpool and the subsequent drive from that city to Wales. He called the number provided by Bill.

"You are in then?" Bill asked Regan.

"I'm not saying that. Just saying let's meet and talk. Not over the phone."

"Okay. Where and when?"

Regan replaced the handset on the cradle and puffed out his cheeks to release tension. He turned to the other man in the room and said, "Okay, Red, it's all set. Next week. I'll pick you up at your place Tuesday at 11 am."

"Alright boss," Red replied as he pulled a funny face and threw a mock salute. Regan ignored his buddy and close friend.

Regan nodded when Red spoke next, "Suppose that means we have a few days off now." It wasn't a question.

THE GLOUCESTERSHIRE countryside was home to Red. He grew up and still had family there including his father. He hadn't been close to him when younger but now his father was ailing in health, Red spent more time with him – whenever the undercover work permitted. Red's partner for the past five years, Jenny, understood. She was that kind of woman. Regan had got to know her well and often thought he should find a woman like her. "Have you got a sister," Regan once asked Jenny. "No, only two daughters but too young for you, so stay away Regan," she laughed.

This break gave Red another chance to be with his father. He always called his father 'Fred.' There was no reason to that. It was simply fact.

"Hey, Fred," Red called out through the letterbox of the Forest of Dean house with its pebble-dashed walls. His father had lived there for forty years. These houses were built in an era when size mattered. The house was roomy by any standards. The gardens, both front and back, were also generous. Red's father had always worked on the land before ill health prevented him from any kind of daily toil.

Fred had no money worries. He owned the home he lived in. He had paid off the mortgage arranged for him by the previous landlord and landowner. It had been a tied cottage, like all the neighbouring homes, but the owner knew Fred was an asset, so he allowed him to buy the home he had previously rented.

Few men who work the land dream of owning their home. So, Fred was surprised when his boss, the landowner made the offer. He was also worried because he did not understand. Fred contacted an old friend, Jack, to advise him. They had known each other from schooldays. They clicked despite their very different personalities. Jack left school and became a civil servant with a government department. Fred worked the land getting his hands dirty. Jack advised him to proceed saying, "It was a great opportunity." No one knew of this arrangement except for the landowner, Jack, and Fred.

Fred heard Red's call at the front of the house. "Is that you, son?" wheezed a response. Fred was a three pack a day man. Red's father opened the front door to let Red in. Turning back down the narrow hall, Fred said, "Tea?"

They sat in the kitchen drinking tea. Red gazed out of the kitchen window to the overhanging sycamore tree.

"It needs pruning."

A few coughs were followed by a nod and Fred replied, "Yes. It's getting out of hand."

"Any petrol in the chainsaw?"

"Yeah, but don't bother. I'll get around to it." Fred coughed and spluttered some more. Red ignored his father as the response was bravado and pride on his father's part.

Red fired it up and the old chainsaw roared into life. As he looked around for the ladders, Red slipped on a moss-covered paving stone.

Fred heard the commotion and wheezed his way to the back door.

"Oh my God," was all he said.

The paramedics arrived to find Red prostrate on the grass lying in a pool of blood, his left arm severed at just below the elbow. Red was alive but with the weakest of pulses. It took the paramedics fifteen minutes to reach the emergency department where Red was rushed straight to the operating theatre.

Chapter 13

RICK GREEN CALLED REGAN to tell him about Red.

"Fucking hell, boss! Stupid bastard!"

"Look, take another week off. Go see Red when he can receive visitors ..."

"Fuck no. I gotta take care of business. The show must go on and Red would agree with me on that score. I know he would."

REGAN PARKED THE VAN next to the shiny clean rental car. The driver of the car had flashed the headlights three times. Regan knew the driver was Bill. The meeting had been arranged for Epsom Downs, the home of England's famous horse race – the Derby. A large unmade car park accommodated both van and car in addition to several delivery trucks with drivers taking their mandatory break.

Bill sauntered across to the van parked nose in overlooking the magnificent view of Central London to the east, Heathrow to the north and the Hogs Back to the west. Neither Bill nor Regan were in the mood for touristy views.

"Where's Red?" snapped Bill.

"Cut his fucking arm off with a chainsaw."

"You're kidding me, right?"

"Do I look like I'm joking?" Regan put on that stone face look – the don't fuck with me look.

"Sorry. Tell him I hope he recovers soon."

"What? As in grow another arm?"

"You know what I mean."

"Yeah, sorry, I'm still shocked about it."

"I bet."

"Where's Blue, anyway?"

"Gone to Miami. Seeing to business."

"I see," Regan said. "Okay, fuck all the small talk. What's the deal?"

"You got a passport?"

"No."

"Get one, pronto. I need you in Miami in two weeks."

"No problem. But what about the visa?"

"You limeys don't need one. You're good to go on arrival Stateside. Here, take this."

Bill handed Regan a slip of folded paper. "Don't bother reading it now. It has a time, date, room number and motel name in Miami. Be there. Likely someone will meet you at the airport but this is just in case."

"But what about the product?"

"Change of plan. You are going to meet the main people. If it all goes to plan, you will be rich beyond your dreams. I take it that interests you?"

"See you in Miami," Regan said extending his hand towards Bill. They shook hands - a firm handshake.

Regan looked into the side mirror of the van. He watched Bill drive away off the car park and turn left towards Epsom. He decided to stay a while and dream. Those same dreams returned. This time they were daydreams. The same fast cars, beautiful blonde, a life of leisure and no money worries.

Why not? Why should it be some other asshole and not me? It's not as if I'm forcing druggies to use the crap. That's up to them. Besides, my piece of the action is far removed from the street. No more debt. No more worries. I can tell the bank manager where to stick his overdraft. What overdraft? The bastard won't give me one!

"Fuck it. I'm gonna do it. Go rogue," Regan's own words disturbed his daydream.

Then the argument commenced in his head.

You will end up in jail, he thought.

"I can do the time," he answered his own thought out loud.

What about your Mum and Dad? They would be devastated.

"I knew you would say that!" he yelled back at the questions and accusations running through his head.

Regan's father had been a cop for twenty-five years. He was proud of his old man. Although they had their differences, they were close after a fashion.

"He will get over it," said Regan to no one in particular, but thoughts were still racing through his mind.

What about Mum?

A tear rolled down from Regan's eye. "Oh fuck me! Why mention her?"

Steve Regan was the first born. His mother had always doted on him. She could see no wrong in him even when he did wrong. Regan loved his mother and could not countenance the thought of her crying if he ended up in jail. So, he dismissed the thought from his head with the same speed it had entered. The tears dried up.

"BOSS, I NEED A PASSPORT and need it double quick."

"What for? Where are you going?" asked Green.

"Miami, Florida, the United States of A!"

"Over my dead body!"

"Bang! Bang! You're dead," Regan pointed a make-believe gun and pulled the make-believe trigger twice.

Three days later Regan held his new passport in his hand. "Hey boss, I don't know how you do it but that was rapid."

Rick Green fired back, "You don't want to know. Come in my office, Steve."

As Regan eased into the leather high-backed chair and stretched out his long legs, Green closed the door behind them.

"Uh uh! I've seen that look before. I could be in for a bollocking."

"No bollocking, but I do want a serious chat."

"That's even worse. A bollocking I can take, but seriousness ..."

"Steve, shut the fuck up ... please. And take off those sunglasses. I bet you sleep with them on."

Regan removed the Aviators and said, "Sorry boss. Go ahead."

"I'm concerned about this trip ..."

Regan's mouth started to move ... "Shut the fuck up." Green cut off Regan before he could utter a word.

"These guys are serious players. Fucking Colombians ...."

"Bolivians actually, boss."

"Same fucking thing. They don't fuck about. This isn't our guys making acid here. These are the real deal. Nasty fuckers. What really worries me is you are going in alone now that Red is off the scene."

"In some ways that's better."

"How so?"

"These guys are gonna be wary of a twosome. It's kinda like classic Starsky & Hutch stuff, don't you think? Besides less chance of cock-ups if I go alone."

"Yes, there is that to be said for it but how are you going to keep in touch?"

"I'm not. Too risky."

"Take a wire with you," Green said.

"No fucking way, boss. Those things are the size of house bricks. I'm dead if they pat me down and find that thing and the wires. Besides you need half a ton of sticky tape to stop it falling and hitting the floor with an almighty bang. 'Oh, fuck me!' says I – 'where did that come from?' No way!"

"I have to agree with you on that one. Promise me this – as soon as you land back at Heathrow, call me."

"Promise."

"And don't do anything stupid."

"Such as?"

"Just behave, is all."

"You sound like my dad," laughed Regan.

"Fuck off, Steve. Who would want you as a son?"

"My mother?"

Green erupted in laughter, "You have always got an answer."

"Let's hope that is always the case. It may just keep me alive."

"Bon Voyage, Steve, bonne chance."

"Ca Va! Et au revoir."

Chapter 14

MIAMI, OCTOBER 1976

MIAMI INTERNATIONAL Airport seemed to be always surrounded by cumulus nimbus. Those huge hammerhead clouds signifying thunderstorms were close at hand. Humidity and thunderstorms go hand in hand. Steve Regan walked towards the glass sliding doors of the airport. Whoosh – they opened as if by magic and whoosh Regan felt wet. Not just wet but soaked. Within seconds his shirt stuck to his back. He had never experienced such humidity.

"Like being in a sauna," Regan said to his driver.

The driver of the white stretch limousine ignored him. His task was to meet Regan and drop him at the motel. He wasn't paid to talk. Besides, he knew talking could get you in trouble with his bosses.

"Talk to me fuckin' self then," Regan mumbled. The driver did not hear or chose to ignore the Regan cussing. Instead the driver, who reminded Regan of a Mexican featherweight boxer in looks and physique, took the bag containing Regan's belongings and placed it into the trunk of the limousine with its mandatory black tinted windows.

This is the life, thought the undercover cop. I really could get used to this. But not the friggin' heat, as he wiped the sweat from his brow and pulled his shirt away from his sticky back. As Regan climbed into the first row of seats behind the driver, he felt the contrast. The air-conditioning of the vehicle had been set at 60 Fahrenheit. Boy, this is good. Cold, but good. Regan was equally as impressed with the stealth of the limo as it purred away from the terminal. He was unable to detect any engine noise, only the swish of the tyres on concrete. Regan glanced up and saw the breeze making the fronds of the palm trees dance.

It took around forty minutes through heavy traffic to arrive at his destination, a beachfront full-service condo overlooking Miami Beach. Steve Regan checked in, immediately feeling comfortable in his new surroundings. Sure beats Blackpool, was an idle thought.

The bell boy carried his solitary bag to Room 620 and gained access to the room. Regan stepped inside. It wasn't a room. It was a suite with a large living area, a kitchen/dining space, large bedroom with a king size bed and best of all a huge balcony overlooking the ocean. He tipped the bell boy a one-dollar bill and received a cheery, "Have a nice day!" Regan thought, They really do say that here, and grinned.

There was a large TV set so Regan pressed the red button on the remote and it flickered into life. He spent the next five minutes zapping through the multitude of channels. He never knew so many existed. The unfamiliar but typical American ring tone of one drawn out ring of a nearby phone drew his attention. Regan found it a contrast to the British trill-trill sound. Just like in the movies, he thought.

Picking up, he spoke into the mouthpiece, "Yes."

It was Bill. "Listen, Steve, get settled in buddy. It's a long flight and you must be whacked. Let's meet and talk tomorrow after breakfast. I will send a car for you."

"No argument from me."

"One more thing. Do you want some company tonight?"

"What do you ...."

"What do you think? You want a girl for the night?"

"No mate. Thanks, but as you say, I'm whacked."

"Okay but the booze is in the fridge. It's all on the house so enjoy. Same with room service if you get hungry." The line went dead.

Regan used the telephone to order room service. A cheeseburger the size of a small loaf of bread defeated him. It was too much even for his voracious appetite. He finished off all six cans of beer and fell asleep fully clothed on the giant sofa in the living area. It was eight in the evening local time.

He woke, startled, at exactly two the following morning and could not get back to sleep. "Bloody jet lag," he said out loud to no one as the room was empty. He carried on with the monologue. "Time to shower."

Pow! Regan could not believe the force from the shower head. "What the fuck!" He yelled again, "How do they do that?" Now acclimatised to the force of the water, he soaped up and spent the next ten minutes in the shower. *I could really get used to all this,* was his overriding thought.

Regan wiped the bathroom mirror with the towel and surveyed his face. He looked younger and cleaner and not because of the soap and water. He thought it best to dispense with the hippie look. Not entirely but tone it down some. His hair was now cut shorter but still hung well over his collar and the beard had vanished. A droopy Mexican-style moustache still adorned his top lip.

Steve Regan spent the remainder of the night watching old movies, Once more mesmerised by *High Noon*. No matter how many times he watched that film, he never tired of it. He first watched it at the cinema in Liverpool. He was no older than ten when his parents took him to see it. They were both film fans. Regan started to think about his mother.

Mum, I hope you understand. If I go rogue, please don't disown me. I love you. It was now daybreak. His chest rose and fell, and he started to sob. His soul was troubled.

A few moments later Regan snapped out of his introspection, once more talking to no one save for his inner self, "Fuck this! Get real or you're going to fuck up big time, Steve."

"Shower, Mister Regan?" No, he thought, the air conditioning had made sure he hadn't sweated up, just a roll of the deodorant and he was fine. He threw on a linen shirt and slid into a pair of chinos, checked the breakfast menu and dialled room service.

"Two eggs over easy on some toast. Orange juice and .... Yeah, okay, tea please." Regan was pleased he remembered how to order the eggs. Eggs over easy or eggs easy over? I must have got it right otherwise the waiter would have laughed, thought Regan.

He took breakfast on the balcony. Before the waiter left, he sipped the tea and spat it back into the cup. "That's bloody awful. Gnat's piss!"

"Would you prefer coffee?"

"I'd prefer alligator piss than that stuff. Yeah, coffee please."

Lesson learned – when in America, drink coffee. Regan liked the coffee served up to him in a large stainless-steel pot. He quaffed his second cup smoking his third cigarette of the morning, gazing on the tanned female forms lazing on the beach below. Blonde, gorgeous, long legs, but do they have money? Regan mulled the question over in his head.

The now familiar drawl of the ring tone sounded again. Regan slowly walked back inside and picked up the handset.

"Thirty minutes. Your driver will be there to collect you." It was a voice unknown to Regan, a heavily accented voice, not quite Mexican, more South American.

The elevator took Regan down to the ground floor. On the way down he thought, Why first? What happened to ground floor? Bloody Yanks! He dropped his room key at Reception and wandered through the cool air-conditioned lobby to take a seat outside the front entrance. God, it's humid, was his first thought as the wet blanket of air smothered him. Fuck it, I need a smoke.

Regan, as many nicotine addicts do, braved the elements to puff away at his cigarette. Finished, he extinguished it in the sand of the chrome stand of an ash tray which doubled as a trash can. With his back to the parking area, he heard the car horn honk twice. He turned to see a Mercedes Spyder pull up alongside him. A window powered down and the same South American voice spoke, "Senor Reegun? Hop in."

He felt like correcting the pronunciation – *Raygun* not *Reegun* – but instead he said, "Nice wheels." He meant it.

There was no response from the driver, no verbal response, only a chilly stare. Regan was learning quickly. He shut up and enjoyed the ride, taking in all the sights on the way. They forced him once more into imagining his alternative lifestyle, the houses, cars, money and women. The twenty-minute car ride gave him many glimpses into what was possible. Possible? Yes, Regan's thought patterns kicked in once more, I can do this. Only cocaine can give me the money I want.

Chapter 15

THE MERCEDES WHISPERED along the boulevards. The hush was sustained all the way to a pastel pink coloured high wall topped with razor wire and bristling with cameras. The driver honked the horn twice, one long and one short. The solid metal gates slid back on their runners ending in a 'clang' as the gate struck the stop point.

The car inched forwards at the same time as the driver powered down his window.

"One guest," said the driver.

The security guard gripped his machine pistol with one hand and saluted with the other. It wasn't a formal military salute but more of a mock salute as between amigos. Regan felt his buttocks tighten. This is serious shit, my man, he thought. It was about one hundred yards of gravelled drive before reaching the large, pink Frank Lloyd Wright inspired house. Regan saw the three Dobermanns and the armed security in the grounds of the house. There were more cameras adorning the front of the building, no doubt all relayed to a central bank of monitors within. A glimpse to his right revealed a helicopter landing pad. Shit! This is real heavy.

The Mercedes came to a stop outside the front door. The door was huge and made up of two identical solid hardwood doors. One of them opened and a familiar face appeared.

"Steve! So good to see you again."

"You too, Bill."

Both men hugged for a moment until Bill spoke again.

"Follow me. I will introduce you to the team, as I call them. By the way, glad you smartened up some."

Regan nodded and brushed his hair back with his hand to check the new length. He followed Bill down a large hallway. On the right was a wide spiralling staircase. To the left more rooms. They went through an open plan kitchen area leading to a three paned sliding door that led out to the pool at the back of the house.

Poolside sat three large round glass topped tables complete with parasols. Each table was surrounded by six comfortable padded high-backed chairs. Further down the pool were several loungers with topless female bodies draped on each one, some showing white cheeks, and some who were gazing upwards, showing tanned tits. Bill's voice made him snap out of his thoughts.

"How is Red?"

"Lost his fucking arm so I guess he's pissed-off."

"Better than losing his head," someone interjected.

Regan wheeled around towards the direction of the voice.

There were three men sitting at one of the round tables. All looked dark skinned with olive complexions and shoulder length black hair. All three wore near identical clothes, white loose linen trousers and wildly loud Hawaiian shirts. Gucci loafers were the footwear of choice. All three men were bedecked in heavy gold – bracelets and neck chains. It appeared they all wore Rolex wrist watches.

The fattest of the three was facing Regan. He was about to insert a lit, fat Cuban cigar into his mouth after addressing his newly arrived guest. His jaw dropped when he heard what Regan had to say.

"That supposed to be some kind of a joke, my fat friend?"

"Sit down, Carlo!" Carlo was about to respond to Regan's jibe until commanded to remain seated by the man next to him. Regan looked at the last speaker who by now had stood. He ambled rather than walked towards Regan with an outstretched hand.

"I am Enrico. You are a welcome guest in my home. Take no notice of Carlo. Sometimes he's an asshole."

Everyone present laughed, except Carlo.

Regan accepted the hand. They not only shook hands but embraced for a fleeting moment. It was long enough for Enrico to whisper, "Be careful, my friend. He will not forget that."

Bill interrupted, "Guys, this is Steve Regan, the Brit I was telling you about. Steve, you have already met Carlo and Enrico. This is Marvin. He is our man in Bolivia."

"Hi, Marvin."

Marvin did not respond except for the smallest wave of his right hand as a gesture of salutation.

Regan knew who called the shots as Enrico ordered the girls to go do something even though they weren't in earshot of any conversation.

The tallest of the girls stood, smiled and said, "Enrico baby, it's too hot to play tennis."

Enrico smiled back, "I hear you Laurie, here baby." He beckoned Laurie towards him. Regan took her in. All of her from head to toe. Laurie was about five feet ten inches tall and slender, but with large tits. She wore nothing but a G-string. Regan thought, Yes. Yes, I could.

Enrico spoke to Laurie again, "Take the girls to the mall. Buy some clothes or something." He peeled off a handful of one hundred-dollar bills and gestured for her to come get it. She walked like a model and took the money. Enrico smacked her arse as she walked away giggling. The girls went inside to get changed leaving Regan, Bill, Carlo and Marvin seated at the round table.

Enrico pressed an intercom buzzer, "Bring more ice and the liquor cabinet." He turned to the men at the table and said, "Okay, let's start again. What happened to your buddy, Steve?"

"He had an accident with a chainsaw. Cut off his arm and nearly died."

"Carlo, apologise to the man," snapped Enrico.

"Yeah. Sorry ... didn't mean anything ...."

"Okay, apology accepted. You're not fat. Just need to go on a bit of a diet," grinned Regan.

Three men laughed. Two did not but stared at each other – Carlo and Regan.

The liquor cabinet arrived. It was wheeled down from the house by a waiter dressed in a white top and black trouser uniform. He looked immaculate. The cabinet was similar to those on an airliner except it was gold plated. The waiter opened it up and removed an ice bucket, tongs and an ice pick along with a large bag of ice. He used the ice pick to break up the ice then tipped it into the bucket. Six bottles were placed on the white linen tablecloth covering the table. Regan could see they were the finest single malt Scotch whiskeys, an Irish whiskey and some bottles of bourbon.

The waiter went about his business in silence and was the epitome of efficiency. He was then dismissed by Enrico.

Enrico spoke first after the drinks had been poured and ice administered. "Let's talk business." It wasn't a request, more of a command.

"Before we do may I ask something," Regan said.

"Sure," replied Enrico.

"Bill, where's Blue?"

"Back in the UK. He stayed to fix the connections over there in case, and in the hope, you decide to join our venture."

Before Regan could open his mouth, Enrico spoke, "We can get to that later. First, we need to know if you are in. To answer that you have to know what you are getting 'in' to."

"Sounds about right to me," replied Regan.

"Excuse me?" Enrico asked.

Bill interpreted, "Just a Brit expression, Enrico. Means he's agreeing with what you just said."

"Why didn't he say that then?"

"I did," laughed Regan.

Enrico showed no emotion, for a second, then burst out laughing. "You Brits crack me up."

Enrico Bruno spoke with a strong New York accent. He was second generation of a Sicilian immigrant family. Carlo Vitale was his cousin and a trusted consigliere. He also acted as an enforcer when required. He and Enrico had been inseparable since they were kids in Little Italy, Manhattan. Marvin Ledesma was Bolivian. He procured the virgin cocaine from the farmers' cooperative in Bolivia and was the conduit to its supply to the Bruno family. The supply route was initially from Bolivia to Miami by small light aircraft. The cocaine parcels, wrapped in oilskin, were fished out of the sea by small fast boats which soon disappeared into the myriad of marinas and docks scattered all around Miami.

These men never went near the product. Nor did they physically handle the money. It was laundered through legitimate businesses. They organised it, controlled it, took the profits and got rid of any obstructions in their way. They were never content, always looking to make more money, find new outlets and satisfy an ever-growing worldwide demand for their product. Enrico knew Europe and the UK were hungry for his product. He saw Regan as the answer to his man in the UK, never quite having trusted Blue. Enrico knew he needed Bill for other things. Bill was busy enough with the supply lines into Miami and Vancouver.

Bruno's crime syndicate was the kind of thing Regan aspired to combat even in his earliest days on the job. He was an idealist when he first became a police officer, thinking he could help change the world by fighting crime. He saw himself as a kind of superhero without superpowers or a cape. He knew society needed laws and it needed the likes of him. Over time he became disillusioned. He was surrounded by incompetents, lazy uniform carriers and some corrupt officers. Moreover, he was surrounded by paperwork, the bane of his life. He soon noticed that many of the incompetents were moved out of the field but upwards, a promotion and more money. Money or lack of it was a constant problem for Regan.

His rapid rise as a star among the detective ranks saw him recruited for undercover work. There was no training, no assessment. Someone thought of him and he was asked. Regan loved the adrenaline rush, so it took no time at all to agree. At first, they were mundane undercover tasks, more like surveillance than deep undercover work. Then he was asked about the infiltration work. Once more, not much thought was needed despite the inherent dangers. He was a natural. Regan had an ability to blend in. He was a human chameleon. He stood six feet two inches tall but despite his height still merged into the background. Regan had those hooded 'Robert Mitchum' type hazel eyes that constantly gave off an aura of chill, as in relaxed. Many women found his looks attractive with his fine chiselled features and especially since his hair grew longer commensurate to the time he spent undercover.

Regan's real family name was also Irish. He was brought up in Liverpool by an Irish Catholic family. His mother Khaterine and grandmother Janet were the driving force behind the family's Catholic values. Both saintly women but tough as old nails. Steve, for that was his real given name, never gave much thought to his faith when growing up in the bosom of the family. It wasn't a subject for discussion but was there, always there, and part of his fabric as a human being. In spite of that, faith did depart him at one stage of his life.

Steve Regan in his private life had once been married. He married his childhood sweetheart, Sarah, when they were both twenty-two years old. One year later Sarah gave birth to Rose. Another year later Steve was a widower. Both wife and baby daughter were killed in a car accident on the outskirts of Liverpool. He ranted and raged at the world and denied the very existence of a god.

Regan threw himself deeper into his undercover world. He became more committed than ever to right the wrongs of the world. His undercover world was where he hid. Regan did his best to isolate himself from reality and became more like the Regan he portrayed than his real self. As much as he tried to hide from reality, once more his real self was threatened when he received news about his mother's illness. She had a tumour on her brain and it was said to be inoperable. The doctors gave her six months to live. Khaterine turned to her faith and enlisted her son's help. He, reluctantly, agreed to accompany her on a pilgrimage to Lourdes in France. Regan was given compassionate leave.

It was during his time at Lourdes Regan regained his faith. It took him by utter surprise. He had taken on board all the doctors had told him about his mother's tumour. He was resigned to losing her as an inevitability. His place was to be with her, to offer support and comfort. A mass was held every day during the weeklong pilgrimage. Prior to one of them, his mother's parish priest, Father Desmond, asked her if she wished to receive the sacrament of the Anointing of the Sick. Naturally, she said "Yes." The priest turned to Regan and asked the same question.

"I'm not sick or dying, Father."

"No, son I'm sure that is correct but you don't have to be. As a carer for your mother you are in need of the Lord's succour and the sacrament also reminds us that God wants to give comfort to the suffering and wants us to relieve suffering where we can."

Regan shrugged and said, "Okay."

The ten o' clock mass was said and both Khaterine and her son were called over to the side of the church. There were ten in the group.

To each in turn Father Desmond anointed them by making the Sign of the Cross on the forehead with the Chrism and said, "Through this holy anointing may the Lord in his love and mercy help you with the grace of the Holy Spirit. Amen." He then anointed all on the hands, saying, "May the Lord who frees you from sin save you and raise you up. Amen."

Regan experienced a feeling he had never known previously. One moment he was aware of his surroundings. He had been staring at the church walls and the Stations of the Cross. Next moment he was in another world. Regan lost focus. He couldn't see. There were only vague images and they were out of focus. It was an out of body experience in which he seemed to regress to the womb and felt utterly cleansed. He felt brand new, clean.

The experience also had an impact on Regan's mother. Within three months of arriving home from Lourdes, the doctors had no scientific explanation why her tumour had shrunk to the size of a pea. Khaterine turned to the open-mouthed doctors and said, "Faith cannot be explained by science." The medical team advised a further scan six months ahead. That scan revealed it had disappeared with no trace. That was two years ago.

Regan concentrated on the here and now of Miami. He reminded himself where he was and who he was surrounded by.

Chapter 16

ENRICO SNAPPED HIM out of his thoughts, "Steve, me and the guys have to go talk in private. I'm sure you understand. We will be back soon and lay the deal out on the table. Capiche?"

"Yeah, I understand. Okay if I take a dip in the pool?"

"Sure, why not? There are some clean Speedos in the cabin over there. Don't pee in the pool, right?" Enrico winked and laughed.

Regan found a locker in the cabin with several pairs of clean swim trunks. Another locker contained one and two-piece women's bathing attire. He pulled on swimming shorts that fitted perfectly, then showered before swimming six lengths of the thirty-yard pool. Regan clambered out of the pool on to one of the recliners the girls had earlier been using and soon dozed off, but not before thinking of Laurie.

His dreams turned to his mother, how the tumour had returned and once more the doctors gave her no hope. Khaterine was a fighter, though. She had discovered there was one hospital capable of giving her hope. The lead doctor had pioneered a new method of micro-surgery and the results were startling. There were two problems. The procedure ran into the thousands of dollars and the hospital was in Boston, Massachusetts. Regan felt compelled to do something about it and help his mother regain her health. For months he wrestled with how to raise that kind of money. The answer was staring him in the face – drugs, and cocaine in particular.

Even though he knew the answer he constantly agonised over the rights and wrongs. It gave him sleepless nights.

The large parasol granted shade to the recliner by the pool. It prevented Regan from seeing the shadow of a man. Even in a state of dozing he would have sensed a shadow falling across his face. Instead of a warning by shadow, he felt the recliner lurching sideways and tried to grip the upper side with his hand. Regan managed that but still he was falling. He felt the water and heard the splash at the same time. He was back in the pool, still holding the recliner.

As he bobbed up towards the surface, he saw a face above the water. It was Carlo Vitale, a fully dressed Carlo. Regan's head and mouth cleared the water and he grabbed a lungful of air before he yelled, "What the fuck! Is this a..."

Regan quickly closed his mouth because he had to. He was now back under water with Carlo holding him down. Carlo had hold of Regan by the shoulders, forcing him under water. Regan grasped his attacker's arms but Carlo was too strong. His grip was like a vice. After a few moments Regan felt the grip relax and came up once more to the surface. Forcing more air down his lungs, he heard Carlo scream, "Who the fuck are you exactly? You a cop? You're a fucking limey cop!"

Spitting out water, Regan was about to shout back. Instead he was forced to take another mad gulp of air as Carlo thrust him under once more. Regan clawed at Carlo's arms in an effort to break free but in vain. He felt himself blacking out, his muscles going limp. Regan knew he was losing consciousness fast and sinking. The air above the water line revived him in an instant. He was exhausted and heard Carlo ranting, "Tell me the fucking truth! Are you a cop?"

"No! I am a fucking nobody and I want ..."

Whoosh! Regan was under again. He kicked out for all he was worth but it was useless. There was nothing to kick as Carlo now had Regan forced down by the head and shoulders so Regan's back was closest to the pool floor. Blackness encroached again.

Regan came to on his side facing the same pool but he could feel solid tiles beneath him. He coughed and spat out water then rolled on to his back. Looking up, he saw Carlo, Enrico and Bill. He noticed a strange look in their eyes. A look of concern. Regan thought, I don't get it. Why look worried when they just tried to drown me? Yet he felt inner relief when he heard Enrico speak, "You okay, Steve? I thought Carlo had taken the play acting too far? Thought we had a stiff on our hands."

Regan spluttered, "Play acting? What the fuck are you talking about?"

"We had to be sure about you. As much as Bill recommended we meet you here, he isn't infallible. We all make mistakes. In this business we can afford no mistakes. So let me say sorry for nearly having you killed."

Chapter 17

THE CARTEL OF ENRICO, Marvin, and Bill moved inside to an indoor movie theatre. Regan and Carlo joined them after they dried off and got dressed, which in Carlo's case involved a complete change from his waterlogged clothing and shoes.

Regan took a seat in the front row, a kind of VIP seat wide enough for almost two with padded armrests. The others were seated to his right except for Enrico. He sat next to a small podium on the stage below the huge screen.

"Right, we are all here. Steve, listen up, this is the deal."

Once the deal had been laid out in its entirety Regan knew. He knew what he was going to do. He was free of Red's restraining influence, free to go rogue and send his mother to America for the surgical procedure. No one would ever know except Regan.

Regan was driven to Miami airport for his flight back to Heathrow.

THE BOEING 747 JUMBO jet made a perfect landing in London. Regan caught a glimpse of the new Concorde jet plane in British Airways livery as he glanced out of the cabin window. Then he was greeted by a grey blanket for a sky and a cool misty morning. Regan felt the difference in temperature and humidity as soon as the cabin crew opened the doors for disembarkation. The cool air made him shudder. He soon cleared immigration, then Customs before walking through the arrival area and finding a telephone. Closing the booth door behind him, Regan dialled Green's private number.

"Hi boss. It's me. I'm back."

"Good to hear. All okay?"

"Yeah, fine. I'll see you tomorrow for a full briefing."

Regan thought - As full as I want it to be. "How's the country boy?"

"Red's doing as well as can be expected after a setback or two."

"Right. See you soon."

Chapter 18

RED WAS TREATED AT Gloucester Royal Infirmary. He had undergone ten hours of surgery to re-attach his severed arm. The surgeons had to reconnect tissue, muscle, bone, tendons and blood vessels. They had done their bit, now it was a question of time and the healing process. Red was in post-operative pain and shock and heavily sedated. He had no idea who had visited him, no idea of the hour or day of the week. Red didn't know how long he had been in hospital or what had happened to put him next to death's door.

Red certainly had no idea who was talking to him. He tried to open his eyes but all was a blur. He was unable to focus. But, he heard the voice.

"Red. You maybe cannot hear me but I'm going to tell you this anyway. Your buddy Regan is in trouble. He may not think so yet but he will be in great danger. He may even get himself killed."

Red could not see but he could still think. Was it a person? Was it sixth sense? As Red recovered, he thought more about this warning. It frustrated him that he was still hospitalised and unable to do much at all. Red was in and out of full consciousness because of the morphine. He began to wonder if the warning was drug induced, merely a figment of his imagination. Then like a shaft of light in a dark tunnel, Red recalled something else.

The voice had said, "Bill and Blue aren't who they say they are. They are undercover Customs."

Red was one of the few people who knew how to contact Regan in an emergency. He was groggy but insisted the nurse bring him a portable telephone.

"Thank you. Thank you so much, Red. You are such a good friend to my son. God Bless you ..."

"Make sure he gets the message, Missus R."

Red had always called her Mrs. R for Regan as a security measure.

Regan made a routine call to his mother. He tried to do that at least once a week. Regan's blood ran cold when he listened to his mother tell the tale of Red's phone call and message.

"Yes, Mum. I'll be careful. Don't worry... yes, God Bless you too, Ma."

REGAN CALLED BILL TO set up the next meeting. He had to wait for three days for Bill to arrive in London from Miami, having stayed longer than Regan, in part to avoid travelling together.

"Hi, Bill. Good flight?"

"Yeah, Steve. All okay with you?"

"Never better. Let's do this thing."

"How's Red?"

"Fine. He'll live, the tough bastard."

"Let's meet in Wales. What about Blue's place?"

"Fine by me. Saturday at midday?"

"Cool," affirmed Bill and the phone went dead.

The drive to Wales seemed strange without Red at his side. Without Red, Regan had all the time in the world to think about what happened next. For one, his newfound freedom without his sidekick had taken on a new complexion with the message passed on to him that Bill and Blue were also undercover, but with Customs and not the cops. This news was a game-changer. Regan hadn't a clue as to how it was all going to pan out as he left Lampeter on the drive to Tregaron and Blue's home.

Bill's car, the same one he had driven at Epsom, was parked outside when Regan arrived. It was the only car as Blue did not own one. Regan parked the van behind Bill's car and walked straight through the open front door of the stone two-storey cottage.

Bill and Blue were seated at the large pine dining table in the kitchen. This was the same table Red, Blue and Regan had sat at only a few months ago. Regan pulled out a chair from under the table and joined them.

"Tea, Steve?"

"Nope, I'm all tea'd out. Must have drunk a gallon between London and here and I stopped in Lampeter and had a cuppa. Tempting, though. It has to be better than the piss served up in Miami," Regan laughed.

"Where's the good lady, Blue?" inquired Regan.

"Gone to her mother's for a few days with the kiddie. Her mum has been sick."

Bill was fidgeting with his car keys and announced, "Guys, enough chit chat. Shall we get down to business?"

Both Blue and Regan nodded in agreement and waited for Bill to speak again.

"Steve, Blue knows all about Miami so I'm not gonna go through all that again. The important thing is for you two to work together and make sure everything runs smoothly at the UK end."

Regan said, "Yeah, I know ... we are facilitators. Don't go near the product or the money. Make sure everyone does as they should and if they don't... we step in. Blue keeps an eye on me and me on him. Simple as that, really."

"Simple, yes. As long as you both do your jobs. Let me remind you. All pay phones. No landlines. You use different pay phones each time. You make sure you're never followed. Use dead end streets, roundabouts, to make sure there're no following cops or bad guys. Be wary of your own shadow and stay cool. If you think you are under surveillance drive the wrong way down a one-way street. Fuck the ticket! Better pay a fine than be dead or busted."

"Strange you use the word surveillance, Bill," snorted Regan.

"Why so?"

"It's a cop word."

"It's also in the fucking English dictionary. You should look it up some time," Bill snapped.

Regan banged the table with his fist.

"Time to stop playing fucking games, Bill. And you, Blue. I know you are both undercover."

"What!" Bill shouted. Blue just laughed.

Regan continued, "Try this for size. My boss, Green, asked your boss to gee us along on a cocaine deal to suss out if we were bent. Gone rogue. I know that's true. I also know you both work for Customs. Bill, your boss, Marks, works at Tintagel House. Blue, you are ex-Met, one of those secret squirrel twats with a dead kiddo's identity. By the way, I'm curious. Does your missus know?"

Blue flew at Regan with his fist drawn back and shouted, "Who the fuck do you think you are?"

Regan stooped to his ankle and pulled out the .38 revolver, at the same time knocking off the safety.

"Sit down! Both of you and put your fucking hands on the table in front of you, palms on the table, flat on the table!"

Bill and Blue sat down on the opposite side of the table from where Regan stood. Both placed their arms out in front of them on the table with the palms of the hands facing down.

"Good. Now don't fucking move unless I tell you."

"Steve, calm down man. Let me explain. We still got a great deal here if you use your brains," Bill said in a soothing tone.

"I'm a good listener but this had better be real good."

Bill explained, "Okay, we are all the same crew. I never asked for this and neither did Blue. Your boss asked our boss to find out if you had gone rogue. He was worried you had. Maybe liking the product too much or something like that? I set up the meeting with you, Red, and Blue in Wales that led to you meeting me in Liverpool. So far so good as this was all part of finding out if you were still on the side of the good guys. Then Miami called. Not DEA, not Customs, and not 'old bill.' It was my old contacts. You met them... you don't fuck with them at all. They know who I am. They don't know who you are, if they did you would be dead now. You would have died in that pool. Carlo wanted to. He dislikes you with a vengeance."

Regan said, "Well, how the fuck do you get away with it?"

"Easy, but not so easy if you know what I mean. Customs is more up its arse with paperwork than the police. We grow forests to keep us going in paperwork and sodding bureaucracy. The bosses aren't field wise. Not savvy at all. As long as you show some results they leave you alone."

"Sounds a familiar story. Pray continue ... I am interested."

Bill continued, "Enrico allows me to throw some small fry to the piranhas every now and then. Either people he hates or who fuck up. As long as I am on board with the main thing he is happy. It keeps everyone happy, Enrico and my bosses at Customs."

"This doesn't make sense. Why would Enrico let you operate like that on both sides of the fence?"

Bill threw his hands to his forehead and sighed.

Regan responded to the movement, "Don't do that again. Don't move your hands."

Bill said, "Okay, from the beginning. You might want to sit down. This is going to take some time. My mother is Sicilian. My real name is Di Maria. Guglielmo Di Maria. Guglielmo is Italian for William."

"I do know that, and Bill is short for William. So far this doesn't help."

"My mother was not married. I never knew who my real father was until recently. She fled Sicily with some of her family and they made their way through Europe, ending up in Liverpool where they managed to get tickets to sail to New York. This was way back."

"So she scarpered because she had you out of wedlock, so to speak?"

"No not entirely, although being a pregnant single girl back in the village was a big scandal. It brought shame on the family and as you surely know Sicilians are big on family. But that was only part of the reason for leaving. Her brother, my uncle, informed on some paisanos involved in smuggling. A contract was put out so they all packed a bag and got out of there real quick."

"So you were born in Sicily?"

"Correct, but I was brought up in New York, and then Canada, Vancouver to be exact."

"How did you end up working for British Customs?"

"I was on a student exchange scheme and ended up studying in London. I was fed up with no money and saw a job advert. The rest is history."

Regan's eyes lit up. The penny was dropping.

"I think I know what's coming next."

"Maybe you do. Maybe you don't. Customs knew about my American and Canadian background. My name was changed legally to Morris back in Canada when I was three. I was soon recruited for undercover work, like yourself. My cover name is Bill Mooney. They sent me to Miami to infiltrate the cocaine cartels. At first I was working with the Yanks, but then Customs decided to go freelance. I built up contacts and eventually they led me to Enrico."

"So how did Enrico find out about you?"

"You are maybe going to find this hard to believe..."

"Try me..."

"Enrico is my half-brother."

"Fuckin' get outta here!"

"It's true."

"This gets better by the minute. Carry on..."

"Okay, I had been mixing with Enrico and his crew for about two months. He must have had someone search my stuff when we were in the pool one day. They found an old photo...."

"I don't fucking believe what I'm hearing... you're undercover and you keep a real photo of the real you. Unfuckingbelievable!"

"Yeah, I know, but it was kind of like a good luck charm. It was a picture of two boys, my mother and her husband, my stepfather. The two boys were me and Enrico."

"Happy fucking families! Hip Hip Fucking Hooray!"

"The rest you can guess."

"I don't want to guess. Tell me! But first tell me why you didn't recognise each other."

"My stepfather, Enrico's father, hated me. He beat the shit out of me when my mother wasn't around. He used to yell at me stuff like 'bastard kid' and 'your mother was a whore until she knew me.' All that kind of stuff. Well, she found out and arranged for me to go to live with her friend's family the other side of Vancouver. I was six. Enrico was eight. We hadn't seen each other since then until Miami. How the fuck were we supposed to recognise each other?"

"Okay, back to the photograph of happy, or not so happy, families."

"Enrico and Carlo confronted me about the picture. They threatened me unless I came clean."

"Threats?"

"Threats and torture. Carlo tortured me."

"How?"

"Waterboarding, then electric shocks. They stripped me naked, hung me upside down and connected wires to my balls and nipples. I thought I was going to die anyway so I told them all."

"What do you mean? Die anyway?"

"Either they were going to torture me to death or... look, I would have done anything, said anything to stop the torture. So I told them. I thought, fuck it! A bullet is better than this shit."

"And..." There was a long pause as Bill composed himself.

"And what? So tell me about all the brotherly love stuff."

"I had no choice. You must accept that."

"I don't have to accept a thing. Just tell me."

"Enrico kept me a prisoner for three or four days. In the house you came to. I think he was deciding what to do with me. He sat me down and spelled out the deal."

"What deal?"

"The one we have to this day. I play both sides at once. I help him move the product, setting up deals and finding new markets. I also keep him in the loop if I hear anything about planned busts that affect his operation. At the same time, I keep my bosses happy by throwing them some scraps. Customs thinks they are big fish but they are zero compared to people like Enrico. Customs get, you know... the lower level dealers... the losers, the ones that don't pay up on time. You know the score. The thing is these people don't fuck about. Enrico is connected and I mean connected. He's part of the biggest and oldest family in New York. The word is even Galletti calls him Don Enrico."

Regan pursed his lips, letting out a low whistle, "Now it is interesting."

"That's one word for it. These people are animals. You don't know the whole story."

"Keep talking."

"Enrico needed insurance to make sure I would toe the line. Our mother is still alive and living in California. He will kill his own mother if I rat on him."

"No ... I don't buy that."

"You don't know him. Not only will he kill her, he will have her gang raped by a bunch of hoodlums before they cut her to pieces to die slowly in horrific pain. He told me what would happen in every tiny graphic detail. I wanted to throw up. He would do it."

"His own mother?"

"Yes. His own mother, our mother."

"Fuck me!"

"The thing is he knew I'm divorced and don't give a shit about my ex. The kids, yes, but they are too far from his reach. And he hasn't got a clue about Caroline."

Chapter 19

BILL AND REGAN SCRUTINISED each other's face, each wondering what the other was thinking, what would happen next. Blue hadn't said a word. He sat as instructed with his arms outstretched, palms facing down. His head was slumped on the table as if asleep. He was listening to every word.

Regan had placed the gun on the table within easy reach. His fingers were moments away from the trigger. The safety was still in the 'off' position. During this lull of introspection and analysis, Bill, without thinking, moved one hand to his face. Regan reacted.

"Put your hands back where they were. Both of them."

"Needed to scratch my nose, is all."

"Do it again and you'll have no nose to scratch."

"Got it. Now you know the whole story, what happens next?"

"Next? Let me see... who the fuck is Caroline?"

"She's a London barrister. I suppose you could describe us as an item. I spend time at her place when I'm in London."

"Does she know any of this?"

"Fuck no! She knows I dabble in a bit of coke and she knows I work for Customs. That's how we met."

"Tell me more, especially the bit about dabbling in coke."

"She is fond of it. The coke I mean. One of my oldest friends is a hostess for Air Canada. She regularly flies into London and mails me some of Marvin's product."

"I don't believe this. Mails it to you!"

"To a poste restante address and I collect it from the Post Office. Fake name and I show fake ID to match."

Blue raised his head and spoke without emotion, "Bill, tell me this."

Bill looked at Regan and the gun but answered Blue, "What?"

Blue said without emotion, "Why did you rape Rachael?"

The pine kitchen table was heavy but Blue heaved it up and over, taking the chance that if he was quick enough in moving his arms the element of surprise would prevent Regan clasping his gun. He was right. In the next thirty seconds a lot of things happened and the tables were turned in more than one sense.

Regan's gun clattered to the granite floor of the kitchen. Regan had leaned back in a reflex action at the sight of the table veering towards him. His chair toppled back and he cracked the back of his head on the solid floor. Blue swung a mighty punch at Bill and landed square on Bill's jaw. Bill fell sideways to the floor with Blue almost astride him. Both men started punching each other with Regan concussed and prone on the opposite side of the kitchen. Blue had the upper hand until Bill felt Regan's gun on the floor. He grasped it and whipped it around the side of Blue's head three times. Blue stopped punching. Bill was the first to his feet and he was still holding Regan's .38 revolver, a snub-nosed Smith & Wesson Detective Special.

Chapter 20

REGAN'S HEAD WAS HURTING like hell. He fingered the back of his head and felt the matted hair. Looking at his hand, he saw the blood. Then he looked up to see Bill standing over him holding a gun. My gun, he thought. Turning his neck brought more pain so he was careful not to rush things. Regan turned far enough to see Blue motionless on the kitchen floor alongside the upturned table. Bill had pistol-whipped Blue some more, for good measure.

Bill spoke first, "Now it's your turn to do as you're told but I won't hesitate to shoot you if I need to."

"You won't get away with this, Bill."

"I have so far and I don't plan on that changing anytime soon."

"So what happens now?"

"That depends on you."

"How so?"

"Go along with the Miami plan. Say nothing about it to anyone and let's all make some money."

"Maybe I will. Maybe I won't. Tell me more about this Caroline. How did you meet?"

"What the fuck do you want to know that for? You make me laugh, Steve. Here I am holding a gun and you want to know about my love life."

"Yeah, weird isn't it? I'm a bit kinky that way. Same as you, Bill, raping your mate's missus and all that."

"He's no mate. Blue's an arsehole. His whore girlfriend was begging for it."

"You're a prize cunt!"

"Who's the cunt? I have the gun. I have the product, the money, the connections. My bosses haven't got a fucking clue what I'm up to. I have a smart classy woman who knows all about me and knows how to keep her mouth firmly shut... You know..."

"Caroline knows all about you? I think you left that out of your tragic tale."

"Seeing it's decision time for you, you may as well know the lot. Yeah, she knows all about me. What I do, the whole shooting match, no pun intended."

"And... tell me again - how did you meet such a classy bit of skirt?"

"Promise not to laugh?"

"As long as it's not funny, I promise, scout's honour, dib dib dob."

"I told you. She was prosecuting a big drug importation case at the Bailey. I was the Customs liaison man. We just clicked."

Regan laughed as loud as his throbbing head would allow, "Oh! Stop! My head's hurting when I laugh. That is so fucking funny it's untrue!"

"It is true," Bill replied without sensing the irony in Regan's mocking tone, "Enough of question time. Except for the big one, what are you going to do? Are you in or out?"

"If I say 'out' what will you do?"

"Kill you."

Chapter 21

"GUESS YOU WILL HAVE to kill me then. But I doubt you have the balls to pull the trigger."

Regan saw movement in his peripheral vision. It could only be one thing. Play for time, Regan thought.

Bill said, "You may find out soon enough."

"Nope. You haven't got the balls. Any man who rapes his mate's missus is scum in my book. Cowardly fucking scum!"

Bill lost the calm façade. He raved, "You have no idea what I'm capable of. I fucked her, yeah. Raped her if you like. She loved it. Begging for it. Great tight little pussy too. Waste of pussy on that fucking wan ..."

Blue was on his feet. He did not speak. He roared. It was an unnatural sound. Like a wounded animal he rushed at Bill. The gun spun around following Bill's arc. Crack! It landed square on Blue's temple and felled him like a stunned animal at a slaughterhouse. Once more, Blue lay lifeless.

This has really gone pear-shaped, thought Regan, Red, where are you when I need you mate. His mind was a mass of confusion. Deep undercover work had turned him into someone else. Most of the time it was easy to deal with. Just play along and act the part. But he knew to do that well, he also had to be the part. There was a fine dividing line between right and wrong. That line was not drawn in the sand. It wasn't easy to see. Even when it was visible there were always ancillary questions. What ifs, as Regan called them. He was, of necessity, an officer of the law but also a law breaker. He had standards, but when it suited his role, he was devoid of standards. He was both moral and immoral, honest and dishonest. Many times Regan had thought, who the fuck am I?

At no time in his undercover career had Regan believed he was in serious danger. Not even in the Miami pool. He didn't see that coming so there was no sense of imminent danger. This was different. Bill was a rogue Customs undercover agent who was deep, very deep into a world unknown to most people. It was a dangerous world inhabited by dangerous people. No matter what Bill Morris said about how he became embroiled in it, he was also dangerous. And he now held a gun pointing straight at Regan.

Bill again asked, "What's it to be? In... or out?"

Regan's mind returned to Lourdes and to an image of his mother. He stood motionless for what seemed an age. It was seconds. But that was all it took for him to finally make up his mind. Can I go rogue? He knew the answer.

The words came easily to him as did the images of his mother interposed with the Virgin. Regan said out loud, "Hail Mary, full of grace, the Lord is with thee; blessed art thou amongst women, and blessed is the fruit of thy womb, Jesus. Holy Mary, Mother of God, pray for us sinners, now and at the hour of death. Amen."

Regan heard no words. He heard a loud bang. He fell back holding his torso. His hands clutched at his belly. He felt a warm pain in the middle of his back. I think I've been shot, Ma, was his last thought.

Bill looked down at the two prone bodies. He bent down and placed the gun in Blue's open palm before closing Blue's fingers around the gun and one finger on the trigger. Before he left the cottage, Bill used his foot to roll over Regan. There was no sign of life.

He stared at the large pool of dark blood staining the kitchen floor and oozing from Regan's back.

The Customs man started the engine of the car parked outside Blue's cottage and drove back to London and Caroline Sewell.

Chapter 22

BLUE TOOK IN THE SCENE in his kitchen. It was one of chaos. There was an upturned pine table and three chairs on their sides. There were remnants of smashed crockery and glass splinters spread out in every direction on the cold granite floor slabs. Blue placed Regan's gun on the stainless-steel kitchen drainer when he saw the pool of blood. Then he saw Regan. Blue dropped to one knee and felt the side of Regan's neck searching for a pulse. Nothing!

Blue packed a small bag with a few belongings, remembering to throw Regan's gun in there. He walked five hundred yards to the nearest phone box. He cursed living in a remote rural community. Inside the red phone box, he made three calls. The first was '999.'

"Which service do you require?"

"Ambulance."

The second call was to Rachael's mother's home.

"Hi Rachael. Look baby, don't ask me anything but pack a bag. I'll be there tomorrow. We're going somewhere warm."

The third call was to a number only known to three men. The call was answered deep inside Tintagel House.

"It's me, guvnor. Bill told me you want to speak with me."

Dennis Marks said, "Don't call me guvnor. I'm not a cockney cab driver and you are no longer in the Met. Yes, I do. Rick Green from Operation Perfume has been in touch with me. They are about to launch massive raids so get out of there; you understand?"

"I'm already gone, guvnor .... Sorry, Sir!"

Blue settled his family into a two bedroom rented villa in Northern Cyprus. It was Turkish territory and somewhat safe from the dangers of extradition. Once Blue had ensured his family was safe, he bade them adieu to return to England for one final mission.

IT WAS LATE FRIDAY evening when Bill Morris parked the car outside Caroline Sewell's flat in Chelsea. It had been a long, tiring drive from Wales. Bill keyed in the numbers into the security keypad, once to get in through the communal front door and then again with a different combination to let himself into Caroline's flat. *I must remember to get Caroline to change the number.* Bill made a mental note thinking of security for her and him. There was a note from Caroline on the kitchen worktop. It read –

See you in The Witness Box if you get back early enough. If not SEE you in BED!

Tired as he felt, Bill decided on a shower, change of clothes and to make the effort to join up with Caroline and her barrister friends. He undressed in the bathroom, folded his clothes up in a neat bundle and threw all of them and his shoes and socks into a black plastic bin bag. He knew the routines of this building. Bill knew if he threw the bag into the communal rubbish chute it would be collected the next morning. By two in the afternoon the same day it would be bulldozed into and under tons of household garbage on some London land fill site and would disappear forever.

It was now ten in the evening and Bill decided to walk to Chelsea Embankment to hail a passing black London taxi. He was in luck as no sooner had he reached the corner of Embankment

Gardens and the main road straddling the river, he spotted the tell-tale 'for hire' roof top light of a cab. A quick wave of the arm and the cab driver swung in and stopped.

"Yes guvnor, where to?"

"Tudor Street, EC4."

The driver looked at Bill in the rear-view mirror and asked, "Lawyer, are we?"

Bill grunted, "No."

The driver interpreted that abruptness as a fare who didn't care much for conversation and drove in silence for the remainder of the journey.

The taxi made progress along a quiet Grosvenor Road and Millbank then into Parliament Square heading for Westminster Bridge. The driver slipped on to Victoria Embankment and Bill watched the flickering lights of the bridges across the Thames out of the right-hand side of the taxi. As the cab drove under Waterloo Bridge, Bill said, "Drop me in Temple Place."

The driver held up one hand in acknowledgement but determined not to speak. As the driver went past Temple Tube Station, he slowed to walking pace waiting for Bill to speak again. "Just here," Bill said handing the driver the fare indicated on the tariff meter plus a small tip. "Keep the change," Bill said, but still no response from the driver, not even a wave of his hand.

Bill took in the fresh night air as he made the five-minute walk through Middle and Inner Temple, exiting the grounds of the Inns in Tudor Street. There on the corner stood the Witness Box pub. It was a pub frequented by barristers and the odd hack. The hacks usually congregated in the Olde Cheshire Cheese close to the Daily Express offices in Fleet Street. On occasion, the crime reporters would wander down to pubs like the Witness Box if they needed some inside information on 'the trial of the moment.' Bill walked down the stairs to the lower ground floor as he knew that was where Caroline and her cronies would be merry making after a hard week's work.

Bill spotted Caroline as he reached the foot of the stairs. She was sitting with two women dressed in the same outfit as Caroline, the black jacket and black skirt look that defined their profession. There were also four male barristers dressed in dark suits, wearing collar and ties. All were seated at the large pine table nearest the stairs. The alcohol fuelled laughter was raucous. Caroline looked up and called, "Hi Bill! Over here," then turned to the bar counter and shouted at the barmaid behind the bar, "Pint of best bitter." The bar maid glared back at the source of the commanding voice without a trace of civility in the tenor of the request.

"Get my note?" inquired Caroline.

"Yes, thanks."

"And you couldn't wait to see me, is that it?"

"Yes and no. I also needed a drink."

"Baby, what's the matter? You look stressed."

"Later, Caroline. I'll tell you when we get home. Right now, I need a drink and to listen to all the boring barrister 'war' stories."

Caroline laughed. She knew Bill had been in this type of company so many times she was sure he knew all the standard barrister jokes. That view was strengthened when she heard Bill utter the time-honoured barrister punch line to the question always put to defence counsel, "How is your case going?" Bill, without thinking came straight out with it, "It was going fine until my client started to give evidence." This got more of a laugh amongst the gathered legal types because it had been answered by an outsider.

Bill remained immersed in thought for the rest of the evening. The group split up shortly after eleven and wandered their separate ways towards Fleet Street to catch a bus or hail a taxi. Caroline and Bill sat in the back of a London taxi cab with Caroline regaling Bill about her day in court.

Caroline punched the keypads. Once more Bill omitted to remind her about changing the code to her flat. He had other things on his mind.

On entering Caroline's flat, she said, "You seem edgy tonight."

Bill replied, "Pour me a glass of that wine, please, baby."

She poured one for Bill and one for herself then sat down on sofa. Bill said, "Turn the music up a little, please." Caroline had tuned in to her favourite FM station. He added, "Look, Caroline, we have no secrets, right?"

She answered, "Now you're scaring me."

"I shot a man dead today."

"Oh, baby! That must be awful. But surely the Customs investigation will exonerate you. It was justified, right?"

"I wish it was as simple as that. I killed a cop. An undercover cop."

Caroline Sewell froze, then reacted, "What? Nothing, I mean nothing, can be allowed to link this fuck up with me. It would ruin my career. You have gone too far this time, Bill, too far. I need to think on all of this. Maybe put some distance between you and me."

Bill queried, "Are you saying that's us finished?"

"I am saying just that. I've shunted the whole coke scenario off to Callum. I'm out of that scene. I will not allow anything to stop my career. You understand?"

Bill grabbed the barrister's throat and squeezed, realised what he was doing and released his grip.

Caroline shouted, "Fuck off out of here now! I mean it, fuck off! You are so fucked up, Bill. Playing your games of deceit isn't enough. You have to go kill a cop! You need treatment. You need help for heaven's sake. Go tell them all about it or I will."

Bill said, "Go fuck yourself! You have no fucking idea."

Caroline yelled back, "Fuck off!"

Bill picked up his coat and left the flat. He took a taxi to his flat in Finchley.

Bill Morris brooded all night. He was unable to sleep. Caroline's words "Go tell them all about it or I will," whirled constantly in his head. His only thoughts were, I can't take any chances. How do I solve the problem of Caroline?

Chapter 23

BEING SHOT ISN'T LUCKY. But there were elements of luck involved in the shooting of Regan. He was taken to Aberystwyth hospital where a surgeon performed a six-hour procedure that probably saved his life. The luck was the surgeon had learned his skills with gunshot wounds in Northern Ireland before transferring to his native Wales. It was also lucky that the .38 calibre bullet had pierced his side but owing to the angle of entry it had exited almost as soon as it had entered. It was a messy wound but could have been far worse. If Bill's aim had been true it would have penetrated and the bullet remained in Regan's torso, damaging either the liver, kidney or intestines. Instead, once the bullet exited it ricocheted off the granite floor and embedded itself in a wooden kitchen door below the sink. Owing to the surgeon's skill, he had stemmed the bleeding and sewn Regan's side back together. Infection was now the major concern.

Regan had one single visitor following surgery. He appeared to be a priest. Regan had no recollection of the visit or what the priest looked like or said. When he recovered consciousness, the nurse in attendance handed him a light brown envelope. She simply said, "A priest left this for you." Regan opened it and found a mass card inside. He thought it was from his mother. But inside the envelope, tucked inside the card, was a typed note:

*BILL WILL KILL THE BARRISTER CAROLINE
SEWELL SOON. KEYS ARE FOR THE WHITE BONNIE ON
THE MAIN CAR PARK. GOOD LUCK!*

Regan's mind raced - Soon? Caroline Sewell is in London. I must get out of this place.

The pain seared through his side as he pulled himself up in bed. A lacerated gunshot wound is no fun. Regan had been three days in hospital since he was shot. He only became aware of his situation during the previous twenty-four hours because before then he had been recovering from the general anaesthetic and the strong painkillers. Regan pulled open his hospital gown and saw the dressing on far left of his midriff. As the wound was on the edge of his torso the dressing was affixed to the front side and back of his waist. He raised both arms. Good, they work, Regan thought and repeated the action with success by moving his legs, one at a time.

Need to get out of here, was Regan's main thought. He looked at the hospital bedside cabinet. On top was a plastic jug of water and a plastic cup. Regan had placed the mass card next to the jug. Underneath the cabinet top Regan saw the open doors and the contents inside. They were his clothes and shoes minus the shirt and denim jacket he had been wearing when shot. Regan got a move on and dressed. He tucked the hospital gown inside his jeans, stuffed his wallet in his back pocket then grabbed the medications on the tabletop. He thrust them down into his side pockets along with the mass card envelope with the motorcycle keys inside it. I have no idea if I'm fit enough to ride a Triumph Bonneville, was a thought he soon abandoned. I must … somehow.

Regan walked out of the ward and into the corridor unchallenged. He saw the lift and pushed the call button. Once inside he pressed the button for Ground Floor and Exit. The lift deposited

Regan about fifty yards from the glass exit doors. There was a sign pointing in its direction. Regan turned right towards the exit, attracting some curious glances on the way. He saw an open office door on his right but spotted something else of interest. He saw a leather pilot's flying jacket hung over the back of a chair near to the door and a navy-blue woollen sweater strewn over the jacket. Regan scooped up both and carried them across his arm to the car park.

Regan blinked in the autumn sunlight, shielding his eyes to scan the car park for the motorcycle. He loved Triumphs and the Bonneville in particular. Regan had always wanted one as a teenager but had to make do with borrowing a friend's for a ride out. There it is! Regan exclaimed in silence. He was taken with its beauty just like he had been years ago. It was a T140 model and Regan knew it was only about one year old as it had the gear lever on the left, a move made to comply with new regulations. It also had the newer 750 cc engine mounted in the oil filled frame with another new additional feature – a front disc brake. Wounded or not, Regan was determined to enjoy his new ride. He knew the marque's history right back to the days this machine's predecessors had competed in world speed record attempts at Bonneville Salt Flats, Utah.

Now for the practicalities, Regan thought. A helmet was slung over one of the handlebars by the accommodating owner whoever he may have been. Regan didn't much care at that moment who had left it there for him. He pulled on the woollen sweater over the pastel green hospital gown then put on the leather jacket. Both were a fit, a little loose, but that was no bad thing as it kept pressure off his wounded side. Regan zipped up the jacket high and placed the helmet on his head, fiddling with the buckle until the strap was firmly in place under his chin. He noticed a pair of sunglasses in the top pocket of the leather flying jacket. Wow! Aviators, Regan thought as he placed them under the helmet until they rested in comfort on his nose and ears. He could not resist the glance of admiration in the mirror fixed to the right-hand handlebar. Fuel tap on, ignition on ... this is going to hurt, he thought as he kicked the kickstart. The Bonnie roared into life. The throaty roar made Regan forget all his troubles and pain.

Regan set off from the hospital car park and knew he had to head to London. That's where I'll find Caroline Sewell and Bill, he surmised as he recollected all Bill had told him before the shooting. Regan was soon on the motorway heading out of Wales towards England and London. He glanced at the speedo and saw the ton fast approach. Ninety, ninety-five, ninety-nine then the magic hundred miles per hour mark. The trouble was the wind in his face and torso was too strong at that speed. It felt as if his arms were being ripped off the handlebars but worse, far worse, was the pressure on his wound. He slowed down to a cruising speed of eighty m.p.h. It was fast enough. It also gave him valuable thinking time. By Regan's reckoning he would reach London in a little over an hour once he crossed the Severn Bridge and back into England.

Chapter 24

REGAN KNEW HE NEEDED help. Red was out of the game and Regan himself wasn't fully functional. His mind wandered as the Bonnie chewed up the miles on the straight but boring motorway. A machine like this is meant for bends, he idly thought, disdainful of the largely straight and featureless motorway stretching out in front of him. He shouted, "Think Regan! Think!" The noise evaporated into the head wind buffeting the top of his helmet. He was annoyed at himself for not concentrating on Bill and how to get help.

Regan's mind drifted to past times and people he had met and felt at ease with. One person came to his mind. "John!" he yelled into the wind. He could help.

John Barnard was forty-three years old. He was as fit as the proverbial fiddle. Regan met him when they were neighbours some eight years ago. They had struck up an affinity and an easy friendship. A friendship reinforced by their joint weekly training runs. John had played a big part in Regan becoming fit. He owed John a lot for that. It was this fitness of body that helped Regan despite the booze and drugs consumed as part of his undercover activities. John also taught Regan about mental toughness and how to cope with pain. John was an expert in these things. He was a former member of 22 Special Air Service Regiment, the SAS. At first Regan doubted he was the real McCoy. So many people bragged about belonging to the most famous regiment in the British Army and never once were they a member. Perhaps they did belong to one of the Parachute Regiments, 1, 2 or 3 Para. Perhaps they applied for the infamous SAS selection course only to fail like the majority. But John was for real. He only started to open up to Regan after they had known each other for two years.

John invited Regan for a week away in Savernake Forest, a remote area outside Marlborough in Wiltshire. It was there John taught Regan many new skills including rudimentary survival skills, how to use weapons and mental toughness. They bonded even more during the week. John was impressed by how easily Regan adapted and soaked up the newly taught knowledge. Part of the survival skills was learning all about camouflage. Camouflage was part of the stock-in-trade of an SAS trooper like John. There were just the two of them for one week, so John had to improvise as these skills were usually honed as a member of a four-man SAS patrol. John was as keen to impart this knowledge as much as the student was keen to learn. So John took Regan through all the skills of movement, camouflage, setting ambushes, anti-ambush drills, contact drills and emergency rendezvous skills.

John also had a stash of weapons secreted within the depths of the forest. It included two Browning HP's and a MAC-10 sub-machine gun once used by John in Northern Ireland. With these, John taught Regan the fine arts of providing fire power protection. He demonstrated how each member of a patrol is assigned an arc of fire to cover, thus providing all-round protection for the patrol as a whole. The last man, or 'tail end charlie', was typically armed with a belt-fed machine gun such as a mini as he must be able to put down a lot of covering fire if the patrol was bumped from the rear. Once more John adapted the training for only two people, him and Regan.

The two of them lived in a subterranean world for most of the week in tunnels John had built over a two-year period. They emerged at night in part to escape prying eyes or stumbling on dog walkers or lovers looking for their own secret place. It also instilled an ability to work in the dark, manoeuvre in the dark and use weapons without the help of daylight. They drank water from a river or caught fresh rainwater. They caught and ate animals like small rabbits or mice. They ate them raw. There were no fires. Nothing could give away their location. Regan loved it except for one thing. He was prohibited from smoking. He felt it was a price worth paying to spend a week in the company of a man he admired and from whom he learned a lot.

It was the thought of the Browning High Power that made Regan enthusiastic. It was used in service in the Regiment for over 40 years, and the Browning HP was found to be a reliable and accurate 9mm handgun. John knew it better as the L9A1, its UK military designation. The Browning has a magazine capacity of 13 rounds. It is a single action pistol which means it must be cocked, the hammer pulled back, before firing the first round. For this reason, the SAS would carry the Browning cocked, with the safety catch on, to allow for a quicker draw and fire. John taught Regan all of this until he had mastered its use.

By the time Regan made his mind up to ask John for the use of one of the Brownings, he had reached Membury Series on the M4. Regan's mind flooded back to memories of the meeting there with Bill. Regan called John from a telephone box in the services area. John agreed to meet within the half hour. He heard the anxiety in Regan's voice so had no need to ask questions. In any event, Regan would not have answered over the phone. There was a telepathic understanding between the two men.

John arrived in his beat-up Ford Cortina Mark 2. He parked next to the Triumph Bonneville just as Regan had suggested. John closed the driver's door then opened the rear passenger door. He reached inside and took out a backpack.

"Second thoughts. Before I go anywhere tell me what's going on."

Regan replied, "Look, mate, I really need your help. I've been shot. I need one of those Brownings because I need to fix things."

John spoke in his quiet, unassuming way, giving the lie to his inner toughness, "Think you had better ride with me. I can hear better than on a bloody motor bike." John glided rather than walked but not like a dancer. It was more like a hunter. He was five feet five inches tall and Regan towered over him. John was the more muscular of the two men. He had broad shoulders, muscled arms and legs and a slim waist. In his middle age, he was a testament to a life in the Regiment and staying fit thereafter. John threw the backpack on to the rear seat of the Cortina and both men got in through the front doors.

"Now, tell me the full story," demanded John as he drove off the service area onto the M4 heading for Savernake Forest.

Chapter 25

"OKAY. YOU ARE RIGHT. You do need help." John Barnard was a master of understatement.

"All I need is a gun. I can't show up at my flat to get mine in case... well... you know why."

"Right," said John, "one thing, though."

"What's that?"

"I'm going with you."

"No way!"

"Look, Steve. No arguments. You can't move properly with that gunshot wound. Don't be a friggin' hero. They end up dead."

Regan did not need much time to reflect on the wisdom of John's words, truth was he was pleased his old pal was going to chaperone him.

"Okay, John. It's a deal. You are now my deputy," Regan smiled.

"Right you are, sheriff."

They laughed and sang the verse of *Who Shot the Sheriff.*

John backed the Cortina off the main road next to Savernake Forest. It was about five yards from the edge of the road. John, as ever a man of few words, said, "Wait here. I'll be back in ten." He was in full military mode now so Regan knew better than to interrupt him or disobey orders.

On leaving the car, John pulled at some tree branches, extracted a knife from his belt and cut several leafy branches. He slung them in front and on top of the car so the old Cortina was invisible from the main road. Regan twisted the rear-view mirror to see John's backpack vanishing into the thick undergrowth with John in front of the pack.

In exactly nine minutes, John re-appeared, opening the driver's door. He placed the backpack carefully on the back seat.

"We have all we need in there," said John.

"Do you mind telling me?" Regan asked.

"Two Brownings, three thunder flash grenades and some medical supplies and ammo."

"Look, it's best if we use the bike," said Regan.

"Why?"

"Better in London traffic than this old jalopy."

"Probably right, but I'll tell you what. Follow me on the bike to Heston Services. That way I have some comfort instead of sitting behind your fat arse all the way."

Regan nodded approval as John engaged first gear to drive back to where they had left the Triumph Bonneville. John wound down the Cortina window on leaving Membury Services in order to wave a cheerio and Regan said, "Be careful, John. Don't want you to get arrested for possession of firearms, do we?"

John laughed.

Chapter 26

HESTON SERVICES IS the nearest motorway service area to London. It was built close to Heathrow Airport. Steve Regan arrived at Heston Services a few moments before John. They conferred, sitting inside the warmth of John's car. Regan insisted John open up the backpack and issue him with one of the Brownings. John agreed. Regan checked it then pushed it into one of the inside pockets of the flying jacket. He now felt safer with Messrs Barnard and Browning as his new sidekicks.

Regan spoke first, "Just thought of something important."

John inquired, "What?"

"I don't know where Bill is. For that matter, I have no idea how to find Caroline other than she's a barrister in this fucking big city."

"That's not good." John, as always, the master of understatement.

Regan thought a few seconds before he spoke, "But I do know what Bill's boss looks like. He came to visit my boss one day so I will recognise him. I also know where he works. We can grab him outside his office and make him tell us where Bill is."

"Look, Steve, isn't it just easier to go to the police now and tell them all that you know?"

"Fuck no! You have no idea. It will be hours, even days of interviews. Asking awkward questions. I'm still undercover, remember. We don't have time for all that police bureaucracy procedural bullshit."

"Okay, you have a point. In for a penny in for a pound."

"One other thing," said Regan, "we need a helmet for you. Wait here a mo."

Regan was away for a few minutes before John saw him holding a black crash helmet. "Where the fuck did you get it from?"

"Gave a motorbike courier a few quid for it and he said 'yes' when he saw the gun." Both men grinned.

John said, "Good man. Let's go." The Triumph roared into life again. Regan eased his way into the London-bound traffic using the acceleration slip road then zipped into the overtaking lane. He zig-zagged his way through the traffic on the motorway as far as the Chiswick flyover. It was now 7:30 am and Regan knew Dennis Marks was in the habit of getting to the office about 8:15 every morning.

He knew this from his conversations with Rick. He had learned to remember seemingly unimportant details because he knew they may become important at some future moment. Regan knew time was of the essence. He swerved around, overtook on the inside and outside everything that got in his way - big, red London buses, delivery vans, cars, other motorcycles, pedestrians, cyclists and of course the arch enemy of London motorcyclists - the ubiquitous black taxi cab. It was drizzling. The kind of rain that produces a potentially deadly slick of oil for motorcyclists. The wet road surface also turned the iron manhole covers into miniature skating rinks for the rider on two wheels.

This ride was fuelled by pure adrenaline. Regan was in the zone. He recalled reading an article describing what a racing driver experienced - a complete absorption in the task and a loss of space and time. It was like that. He occupied a space inhabited by no other being until a black taxi cab swerved without warning into the zone previously occupied by Regan alone. The Triumph was alongside the rear offside door of the cab when Regan became aware of the imminent danger. Regan threw his body weight to the right and forced the bars right and down to avoid a collision. John hung on tight.

The cab driver wound down his window shouting, "You fucking idiot!" The irate taxi driver pumped the accelerator pedal to catch up with the Triumph which was held up behind a London double decker bus. The cabbie made the mistake of swearing again at Regan as he pulled up beside him. Regan said nothing. He reached out to the black cab with his left hand, steering the motorcycle one-handed, then grabbed the side mirror mounted on the front wing of the cab. The mounting cracked leaving Regan holding the mirror. He threw it to the side pavement, and he could sense the smile creeping to his ears. Around the bus he steered, twisting the throttle to accelerate away. He was now back in the zone.

Regan stopped the motorcycle on the busy Albert Embankment and decided to wait. Both removed their crash helmets and dismounted. Regan needed a smoke so pulled out his pack and lit up.

"You still puffing away at those cancer sticks?"

Regan ignored John. He had got used to this line from him over the years.

"I think we wait here. Once he arrives, he has to slow down for this junction. That's when we jump him. See the entrance to the office block just there. He has to slow down to enter. Just leave it to me."

John nodded.

The rush through London's morning traffic proved to be a worthwhile cause. Regan discarded his smoked cigarette into the gutter. He looked up and saw Bill's boss, Dennis Marks, driving a dark green Rover saloon. He was alone. The Rover slowed just like Regan had predicted. He saw the front wheels turn towards the entrance and spoke, "John! Go!"

In seconds both men were standing alongside the Rover, Regan at the driver's side and John stationed at the opposite side. Marks turned his head to one side then the other. He did not look at the faces. He only had eyes for the two Brownings pointed at him.

Chapter 27

REGAN TAPPED ON THE driver's window with the gun barrel and gestured in a downward motion. Marks unwound the window a few inches. "My name is Steve Regan. I'm an undercover cop but you already know who I am. We are going to jump in the car with you and go for a short ride. Do you understand?"

"What if I say 'no' or drive off?"

"It will be the last thing you ever do."

Marks looked into Regan's eyes, for Regan had removed his Aviators. Another ploy he had learned from John – when negotiating with the 'enemy,' let them see your eyes. Marks knew the cop was serious. He pulled up the central locking button on the driver's door. No sooner had the button clicked the two men got inside and sat down. John sat in the front passenger seat with Regan in the back right behind the driver, Marks. Regan and John had their weapons aimed at the driver's head. Marks was unaware neither man had released the safety or cocked the Browning SAS-style.

Regan broke the brief silence, "Drive normally and follow my directions. Don't talk unless I ask a question." The Customs boss nodded his head in understanding. Regan directed the driver first to execute a U-turn to head towards Central London. After a few hundred yards, Regan spoke again, "Turn right into Tinworth Street, just there," as he pointed with his free hand in front of the driver's face. "Now, as soon as you pass that pub on the right, turn left into Randall Street.

The next thirty seconds of the drive were in total silence until Regan spoke again, "Pull over right there. You see the parking space about thirty yards ahead on the right? There."

There was no answer, but Marks, the driver, did exactly as instructed. This was a side street occupied by small industrial workshops with rolled steel shutters. They were under the railway arches and leased to small businesses by British Rail. There was no movement in the street apart from two stray dogs fighting over a bone at the end of the street. The only noises were the dogs and the trains click-clacking on the railway track above the industrial units.

Dennis spoke as he pulled on the parking brake, "What is it you want from me?"

Regan said, "Only the truth. I have no time to spare and I need to know where Bill is."

"Bill who?"

Dennis felt the pistol barrel prodded into the nape of his neck.

"Do not fuck around, Mr. Marks. You know who I am talking about. Bill, your agent you sent to Wales to see if I had gone rogue."

Marks said, "Okay, okay, what do you want to know?"

"I need an address for him or even better, his address and Caroline Sewell's."

"What do you want her address for?"

Another prod of the gun barrel produced a wincing noise and left a red weal on the back of Marks' neck. "Right, alright. I got the message. But how do I know you aren't on the other side, gone rogue, gone dark?"

"You don't, but here is how it is. It's your man who is rogue. He shot me and beat up Blue badly. Raped his missus too. Now he's on his way to murder a fucking judge. There's only me and my buddy here can stop him," Regan paused then shouted close to Marks' ear, "Underfuckingstand? Capiche? Dig? Comprendez?"

The Customs man recoiled from the noise reverberating in his ear. His body gave an involuntary shudder. "He lives in Finchley at his flat 23A, Hendon Avenue, Finchley. All I know about his barrister girlfriend is she lives in a flat in Ranelagh Gardens, Chelsea. I remember Bill telling me it had a red telephone kiosk on the pavement right outside the entrance."

Regan calmly said, "Is all this kosher?"

"I swear it is. What happens now?"

"Simple. My buddy will tie you up, gag you and we will put you in the boot of the car..."

"What!"

Regan said, "What what?"

"That's outrageous. It's kidnapping. Look, why don't we go to the office. One phone call and I can call in the cavalry."

"I don't have time for all that. You don't get it. Your man is about to kill a judge any time soon. Besides, your mob will start asking too many questions of me," Regan said.

John reached into his backpack while Regan was talking. He removed a roll of duct-tape, snapped some off and plastered it over Marks' mouth.

"Time to shut up..." said John, "Now twist around in your seat, put your arms behind your back."

Marks complied as John snapped on the plastic cuffs and tightened them, so their prisoner's arms were pinned behind his back. Regan got out of the rear passenger seat and opened the driver's door. He held Marks' shoulder and gestured upwards. The prisoner stood up outside the car. Regan pushed him to the rear of the car where John was using the car keys to unlock the boot. It sprang open. Regan positioned Marks so his back was resting on the rear of the car. One push from Regan and Marks fell into the boot with his legs sticking up in the air. John held both Marks' ankles and twisted so the Customs man ended up on the boot floor mat and his body lay at right angles to the car. In a flash, John snapped another plastic tie around his ankles. Marks could no longer cry out or move his arms or legs. Satisfied, John closed the boot lid.

"What would you have done if he hadn't talked, Steve?"

"Oh, I don't know. Maybe flogged him with a wet lettuce."

"Same weird sense of humour I see," John replied. They broke into a trot after secreting the guns in the backpack.

Regan and John ran back to where they had left the Triumph. There was no time to waste.

Chapter 28

IT ONLY TOOK A FEW minutes of riding the Bonnie for Regan to feel back in the zone. All thoughts of Bill and Caroline were banished in this space. He gunned the Triumph for what it was worth through Vauxhall, on to Vauxhall Bridge and slewing left into Grosvenor Road reaching speeds of seventy miles per hour. He heard the sound of two-tone horns so checked his mirror and glanced behind him. "Oh shit! Just what we need, a fucking cop car. Hold on tight, John."

John wondered what the hell Regan was up to because instead of increasing speed, he slowed down to around thirty. He soon found out. Regan had slowed down so he could glance left and right. He was looking for something. The Triumph dipped down at the front as Regan applied the front brake, forcing John to slide into Regan's back. Then the machine lurched to the right at almost a ninety-degree angle. John saw what Regan was aiming for.

A few seconds later, Regan had reached the end of the pedestrian passageway. It was too narrow for any car, never mind a police car. He looked in the mirror and saw the police car parked on Grosvenor Road at the entrance to the passageway. Regan could not resist smirking.

Several more minutes of riding back in the zone saw Regan arrive in Ranelagh Gardens. The area was occupied by up-market flats. Each building was three storeys high. Where is it? They thought.

"This is the right place, John. Look out for the red telephone box outside a block of flats."

They saw it at the same time. "There it is!" Both men spoke as one.

Regan almost dropped the Bonnie in his rush to speak to a security guard in charge of the small residents' car park.

"Excuse me, mate. Have you seen my friend? Caroline, the barrister. I have some urgent paperwork for her."

The guard was a huge, black guy who appeared pleased to have someone to talk to. His face lit up on hearing Regan's inquiry as if no one ever noticed he was there and now he felt important.

He spoke slowly in a West Indian patois, "Yeah, man, lady left already. You mean the blonde barrister lady?" His accent made barrister sound like barista.

Regan nodded, opened his mouth to say something but the guard continued, "Strange thing is man, the boyfriend left after the lady."

Regan asked, "Why strange?"

"Well man, when the man stay, he always leave with her, always together innit?"

"What does the man look like?"

"Hey man! You ain't no jealous boyfriend or anything, is you?"

Regan burst out laughing, "No way man! She just friend of mine." Regan in his chameleon way started to imitate the patois.

Regan saw the guard's shoulders relax before he spoke again, "The man he ugly. Squashed face, man. Can't see what she see in him. She's a looker, know what I mean."

"Thanks, I think..."

The guard hadn't finished cooperating, "Wait she did say what she doing today. Made a change. She smile for once and had a spring in her step. 'Not far,' she said 'Off to Inner London Sessions. I'm doing a stint as a Recorder.'"

He smiled again before adding, "I made her laugh. I said I didn't know she was in an orchestra. She gone and told me a Recorder was a part time judge. She said she has a trial starting there today."

"How long after she left did the guy leave?"

"Strange that. Only a few minutes. I did wonder why they didn't leave together. It seemed like he was trying to follow her or something."

"Why do you say that?"

"Man, he hid behind that tree down there and watched the lady grab a taxi cab. Then he did the same thing. It was weird, man, like in the films, you know, follow that car," said the guard with a laugh that would have been infectious in different circumstances.

"How long ago was all this?"

"About twenty minutes ago."

Chapter 29

REGAN ROARED OFF ONCE more on the Bonnie with John Barnard clinging to his back. John still had the backpack strapped to him with all the tools of his former trade.

He weaved in and out of the London morning rush hour traffic. Regan felt justified to have chosen the Triumph as his two wheeled pursuit transport in the metropolis. Adrenaline now overwhelmed him and overrode the nagging pain in his side from the gunshot wound. It was just as well because his riding style had to be aggressive but also defensive.

Taxis of the black cab kind and buses are the two worst enemies of anyone on two wheels in London. One black cab tried to carve him up on Chelsea Bridge just like the earlier incident in the race to interdict Marks. Regan swerved to avoid colliding, but this time kicked the driver's door. He was tempted to once again wrench the cab's offside mirror off before throwing it into the dark Thames below. The driver shook his fist at the disappearing exhaust pipes of the Bonnie.

Regan pulled off the busy Elephant and Castle roundabout into Newington Causeway. He knew exactly where the Inner London Sessions Court House was from years back giving evidence in a case there. As he got close, he relaxed the throttle and dropped his speed to around fifteen miles per hour. Both men now had their 'eyes on.' Nothing escaped their attention whether moving or stationary.

"There he is," shouted Regan. Underneath a spreading chestnut tree inside the grounds of the courthouse stood Bill Morris. He was trying to look nonchalant, smoking a cigarette. Even from a distance Regan could see he had eyeballs on the sandstone steps leading to the entrance of the court building.

There were small groups of people and individuals walking towards the entrance. Some were obviously barristers or solicitors. They all wore the same uniform of dark grey suits and carried grand looking bags. It was even possible to say who were the barristers as they carried a cloth bag tied up with a drawstring. Inside, nestled the badges of their profession, a horsehair wig and a liveried tin that protected it, and the black court gown. The tin was embossed with the barrister's initials. The female barristers were even easier to detect. Without fail, all wore the same black jacket, skirt of the same colour and a white high-necked blouse. They also carried the telltale cloth bag.

Regan turned right into a side street alongside the court building and parked the Bonnie. John pulled off his backpack, opened it and checked the contents. First, he checked one Browning, then the other. He handed the second one to Regan who checked it again then pushed it into the large side pocket of the stolen flying jacket. John secreted his inside his belt then both men hid below a low wall in front of a house opposite the grounds of the court. They had a perfect view of Bill who was still leaning against the tree. He was leaning but watching. Regan and John were watching him.

Caroline Sewell had first taken a cab to her chambers to collect some papers before taking the Tube. First from Temple Gardens Tube station to Embankment then on to the Elephant and Castle. From there, she walked the few hundred yards to the courthouse. As she walked through the gate of the court into the grounds, she remembered to use the entrance reserved for judges. It was at the side of the building and close to where Regan had parked the motorcycle. The cab ride to her chambers was unplanned. It had initially confused Bill who thought she was heading directly to the Inner London Sessions. He realised what was happening and decided to wait for her to arrive at the courthouse.

Regan saw Bill stand up straight and followed his line of sight. He saw a tall, attractive blonde walking towards the corner of the building. She walked upright, straight-backed and had a certain elegance about her. He was looking at Caroline Sewell for the first time. She was dressed like all the other female barristers but she was distinctive. Maybe it was the way she walked, thought Regan.

Both Regan and John moved out of their hiding place as they saw Bill follow Caroline to the corner of the building. She was heading for the judge's entrance. They moved quickly but stayed low and both men by instinct had one hand on their weapons. Before setting off, they had cocked the Brownings SAS-style.

"Caroline!" It was Bill who called out her name.

Chapter 30

CAROLINE SEWELL TURNED around and saw Bill Morris holding a gun. She had no idea of the type of gun save it was a pistol he held in the palm of his hand and it pointed at her.

"Armed police!" It was a disembodied voice amplified by a megaphone. It startled Regan. It also made Bill spin around towards the source of the noise. It was a uniformed police officer. The officer spoke again, full of urgency, "Drop your weapon immediately!"

Bill Morris turned back towards Caroline who was frozen in her tracks. She found herself unable to move forward or back, never mind run. Her mind was frozen too, along with all her faculties. She was unable to speak nor scream. He raised the gun once more in her direction. A man in a Stetson with a wild beard jumped out from behind a sycamore tree and fired at Bill at point blank range. Regan recognised him. It was Blue. As Blue pulled the trigger, he shouted, "This is for Rachael." Bill fired once. Blue dropped like a stone.

John reacted despite what he had just witnessed. He pulled off three rounds from the Browning and all hit the target – Bill Morris. He had been trained to ensure all potential danger was eliminated. His military training also meant he knew the effects of different types of weapon and the different sounds they made. John Barnard had heard the snap of a high-velocity bullet and saw its effect on Bill's body as the impact forced the now dead Bill into an involuntarily leap backwards and a macabre dance. A second high-velocity shot rang out. The face of Bill Morris was no longer recognisable as a result of the head shot from the trained sniper on the courthouse roof.

The officer's voice rang out once more, "Drop your weapons, now!"

Regan and John Barnard lowered their weapons to the ground and complied with the next amplified order, "Good. Now get face down on the ground with your hands open and arms above your head. Stay like that. Under no circumstances move again until you are told to do so."

Regan cocked his head to one side to glance at Caroline Sewell. She looked as pale as a ghost. Her bag was at her feet and she was holding her face in both hands. Next, he heard a metallic sound. It was his gun kicked away from where he had laid it, followed by another identical sound of John's gun dealt the same fate.

He next felt a kick in his ribs. Luckily it was his good side not the gunshot wound. Regan kept his cool and lay there motionless. He knew the drill. Plastic ties were placed around his wrists but not before two officers pinned his arms behind his back. More ties were placed around his ankles. Regan felt like a turkey at Christmas time. He could sense hands patting him down and probing all over. Under his arms, behind his ears, his neck, chest, arm pits, back, inside his belt, groin, buttocks, back of his knees, his pockets then a familiar voice but without amplification.

"My officer is now going to remove your footwear."

His boots were pulled off one by one. Then the probing hands checked his stockinged feet and dove inside the boots.

It was then he was yanked to his feet in one swift coordinated movement by two male officers who flanked him.

One of the two said, "You are being arrested on suspicion of unlawful possession of a firearm. You don't have to say anything but ..."

Regan could not resist, "I know the drill."

The same process was repeated with John Barnard by two other officers but this time they managed to finish the police caution about self-incrimination without interruption. Regan was three yards away. He called over to John, "Don't say a word. I will explain it all." For his trouble, Regan was struck by one of the officers with a sly but ferocious dig into his side. Regan spoke no more until they reached Vauxhall Police Station.

Chapter 31

REGAN REFUSED TO GIVE his details when asked by the custody sergeant on arrival in the custody suite. He said, "I am unable to give you my details as to my identity. I am requesting I be permitted to speak to the most senior officer on duty today."

The burly and surly desk sergeant had seen and heard a lot of things in his day but this was new.

"I'll ask the Commissioner of the Met to come, shall I?"

"He will do, but a Chief Super, preferably a Detective Chief Super, will do just as well. In fact, make it a uniform boss not a DCS."

There was something in Regan's tone and demeanour made the world-weary sergeant take notice. It wasn't what Regan had said, rather it was the way he said it.

"Put them in separate cells. I'm going upstairs to speak to the guvnor."

The overweight sergeant was out of breath by the time he climbed four flights of stairs to the boss's office. He paused before knocking at the door to compose himself. The Chief Super called out, "Enter," and looked up to see who was at the door.

"What is it, sergeant ? Thought you would have stayed away from here seeing you have only got three months before your pension. You'd better get a bit fitter, too. You know so many coppers drop dead after retiring."

"That's it, guv. I don't want to fuck up now so close to retiring from the job. I got a feeling about this prisoner downstairs. Kind of a sixth sense if you will."

The sergeant told his boss about the incident at the courthouse and about the two prisoners.

"The thing is, he's refusing to give his name or any details and said he must speak to a senior officer. I got this feeling about it all."

The Chief Super sat back in his sumptuous fake leather chair, then scratched his chin before speaking.

"I'll tell you what. Arrange for an interview room, the one with the listening device. We should record what he has to say. I'll listen to his story... it'll make a change from all this paperwork."

The Chief Superintendent introduced himself before sitting down on one of the metal chairs bolted to the floor of the sparsely decorated interview room. Regan was seated opposite him.

Regan got straight to the point after the introduction. "I'm an undercover cop. Before I tell you the full story let me tell you this. There is a Customs boss by the name of Marks trussed up in the boot of his car. It's a maroon Rover saloon parked in Randall Road. Please arrange to have him released."

The Chief Superintendent weighed up Regan again, displaying the nervous tic of scratching his chin when faced with making a decision.

"No need to tell me the full story, I believe you but you will have to stay here. You know the score. Someone will have to interview you and take a full statement from you."

"I suppose that has to be right. Okay, please arrange that and let me out of here. One other thing tell them to leave John alone. He can add nothing."

Chapter 32

THE DETECTIVES FINISHED quizzing Regan and released him and John. They insisted on first driving him to St. Thomas's Hospital for a check-up where he was given a clean bill of health. While waiting for the various test results, the Chief Superintendent approached Regan and said, "I have some news for you. The judge wants to see you."

Regan said, "What judge?"

"Don't tell me you have amnesia. 'What judge,' my arse. She wants to thank you personally for what you did."

Regan and John got a personal escort from two uniformed officers in an unmarked area car. First, they dropped off John at a small hotel near London Bridge so he could get some sleep. Then they drove on to Inner London Sessions Courthouse, the scene of the crime. But this time, Regan did not have to act in a clandestine manner. Instead he was escorted to the judge's side door. The slimmer of the two officers pressed the intercom buzzer and the door opened without delay. A black-robed court official greeted Regan and said, "Step inside, Mr. Regan, and follow me." The officers remained outside.

Dutifully, Regan followed the official up four flights of steps, two at right angles to the others, until they reached the first floor of the building. Regan noticed the stone steps were worn with the passage of time and the feet of lawyers. He noticed they were only worn away in the middle and at the edge of the tread resulting in a dip of about one inch from extremity to the middle. Regan looked up from the top step and took in the corridor. The passage was wide and the ceiling high. A number of large heavy wooden doors were symmetrically stationed along the length of the corridor. The official stopped and knocked at one door bang in the middle of all the others. He opened it with caution and about an inch so he could peer inside the room.

"Come in," said a female voice, "I was expecting you. Thank you, Frank, you may leave Mr. Regan alone with me."

"Tea or coffee?" the judge inquired.

"Tea, please. What do I call you, Ma'am, judge or what?"

"Caroline. Call me Caroline, please."

"If you insist, but I feel a bit uncomfortable about that."

"Nonsense, Mr. Regan. You saved my life and I want to personally thank you."

"I suppose you are right. What about this? I call you Caroline and you call me Steve."

Caroline Sewell threw back her long blonde hair which she had untied in readiness for Regan's visit. It had the desired effect. That, and her sensuous laugh made Regan think of her naked.

"Steve, I do need to thank you but I have little time to do that properly today. I am in the middle of a trial and during a break I arranged to see you. I am delighted you accepted my invitation."

"Well, the way it was put to me was more of a demand than an invitation," smiled Regan.

Caroline found his smile and demeanour attractive. She smiled back.

"Right. I can assure you it wasn't a demand or a command, merely a request. Will you meet me for dinner Friday evening? My treat, of course."

"How can I resist? It's not every day an attractive woman and a judge to boot asks me out for dinner."

Caroline beamed once more and found Regan's charm irresistible.

"I am only a part time judge. I hope to be a Circuit Judge soon."

"Part time? You make it sound like a supermarket checkout job. What's a Circuit Judge?"

"Allow me to explain all to you over dinner. Hear that bell? That is summoning me back into court. Stay here and finish your tea and Frank will show you out when you are done."

"Right, but where and when do we meet Friday?"

"Do you know the Savoy Grill in the Strand?"

"Yes."

"Okay, 8 pm in there Friday. Don't be late."

Caroline Sewell rose from her chair with the lithe ease of a woman in splendid shape. Regan watched her tie up her hair, gather her lawyer's wig and stride to the door with purpose, poise and dignity. My God, she is sexy, thought Regan.

Chapter 33

THE TIME BETWEEN MEETING Caroline at the court and the dinner date enabled Regan to have a long chat with his boss, Rick Green. They met for lunch in a pleasant and typical English country pub just outside Alton in Hampshire. Green was visiting family nearby and took the opportunity of catching up with Regan.

Green ordered the steak and kidney pie. Regan chose fish and chips with the mushy peas. Over a Guinness for Regan and a pint of bitter for Green, both men dissected recent events.

Green said, "What on earth were you thinking of, kidnapping Marks?"

"Thought you would ask me that. Let's just say it seemed a good idea at the time," said Regan.

"I see nothing has changed. You're still a cheeky bugger. Good job you saved the judge's life or else you could be in jail right now."

"Yeah, I guess," Regan replied, reluctant to be drawn on the episode.

"You are unusually quiet, Steve. Is all okay with you?"

"Fine. Look I don't mean to be rude but I went through everything with the Met. I don't intend repeating it all. Surely you have read the reports?"

"Okay, I'll change tack. You need a few months away from work. Recharge the batteries, so to speak."

"No argument from me on that. How long do you have in mind?"

"No rush at all. You need time to get over the gunshot wound and the trauma over the shooting. Come back when you're good and ready."

Once again Regan played his cards close to his chest when dealing with his boss, Rick Green. He had no intention of telling him he was determined to bed Caroline Sewell.

DINNER AT THE SAVOY Grill between Regan and Caroline was more about mutual attraction than the food. They both played 'the mating game.' It became the springboard for a whirlwind relationship. Regan had been accommodated in a plush Mayfair hotel courtesy of Rick Green and a sympathetic Home Office. After a few weeks of daily contact with Caroline, he moved into her flat.

Chapter 34

MONTHS WENT BY AND it was clear to Caroline that Regan had replaced Bill as her lover with one big difference. Regan was her first live-in, unlike Bill who only stayed when invited. She relished their animal-like love making and appreciated Regan's superior technique compared to her former lover. Regan started to sense part of his goals were fulfilled. He now had a wealthy girlfriend, a Jaguar that Caroline had gifted to him and no money worries because Caroline insisted on picking up the tab for everything. He was in no rush to return to work just like Green had urged upon him. Nevertheless, he felt something. Something not right about Caroline and he also sensed she was dangerous. That was part of the bond between them. It was the same thing that attracted him to undercover work - a sense of danger and adventure.

Regan's sense she was dangerous was reinforced one evening in a bar. A barrister approached Caroline in familiar tones but from a bygone era, "Hi Cee! Got any of that Colombian army marching powder?"

Regan watched from his table as Caroline reacted. She pushed the woman back to the wall, pinning her there with one arm to her throat. She fished in her shoulder bag and found what she was looking for - her manicure scissors. In one swift move she pressed the scissor blades under the woman's eyes and hissed, "What the fuck is your problem? I have no idea what you are talking about. If you don't shut the fuck up you will lose an eye. Got it?" The woman flung her hand up to her cheek to wipe the trickle of blood away. Caroline had pierced the skin under her left eye.

"I got it. You're a fucking lunatic. Let go of me!"

Caroline released the frightened victim who scurried out of the bar exit doors into the street. Regan watched bemused as Caroline strode to the ladies' powder room like nothing had happened.

Caroline locked the cubicle door behind her. Her thoughts were scrambled but there was a theme - no one will ruin my career. She idled the time away sitting inside the cubicle, staring at the plain white door with its stainless-steel bolt. Her mind went back to better times with Bill. She recalled deep intimate moments with him and secrets shared between lovers. Bill had told her about his work and Regan's plan to go rogue. He told her all about the cocaine deal and what happened in Miami.

Caroline's thoughts returned to the present and Regan. She calculated the information about her new lover may in the future be useful so decided to keep it to herself. She also knew that could be difficult. Caroline Sewell knew herself well, her strengths and foibles. She knew she was a gossip. She could not resist telling her lovers all about her professional and private life. She suffered from verbal diarrhoea; a useful trait given her profession.

AS TIME WENT BY REGAN and Caroline were still as hot as ever. They became even closer. Caroline was so relaxed in Regan's company her guard had disappeared. She was no longer circumspect about her drug habit or past dealing. Regan was wary but overcome by carnal lust. He loved the intimacy of the new relationship. While the sex was as good as this he had no inclination to analyse things. He wanted her and she wanted him. It really was as simple as that.

Regan and Caroline had dined earlier after Caroline finished her day in court. Indian curry was the joint decision washed down with cold beer. The couple arrived at Caroline's flat soon after 11:30 on the Friday evening. Following routine, she asked Regan to open a bottle of red wine while she showered and changed. Regan poured two large glasses of Caroline's favourite wine, a classic Barolo. He had taken a third sip and stretched out his long legs on the sofa listening to Chopin playing on the hi-fi. He was in for a treat. Regan let out a low whistle on seeing Caroline stroll into the living room wearing nothing save for a G-string panty. Her long blonde hair was trailing down her back as she pirouetted so he could get a better view.

"You are amazing. Such a sexy woman," Regan said.

"I know," Caroline replied as she lay down next to Regan on the sofa. She quaffed a mouthful of wine then unbuckled the belt on his jeans. Caroline pulled on the zipper and tugged at the waist of the jeans. They were down at his knees when she ordered him to remove his underpants.

"You are the boss, Milady."

"I know and you love it."

Caroline's head and long hair disappeared between Regan's thighs. She stopped talking as her mouth was busy. A few minutes of oral massage forced Regan to stop his low moan and speak, "You're going to make me cum."

Caroline came up for air and said, "That's fine. Just get ready to fuck me later in bed," before she continued with her oral massage. Regan ejaculated letting out a loud moan. "That was fucking great. You are a porn star, not a fucking judge."

"And now I'm going to get as drunk as a judge," she said taking a gulp of red wine to wash down the part of Regan he had deposited in her mouth.

"I love it when you swallow."

"Is there any other way?" Caroline smiled, licking her red lips.

She removed his jeans and underwear then lay her head in Regan's lap.

"Let's lie here a while, Steve."

"Fine by me. We have music, wine and each other. Sounds good to me."

"Steve, things are good between us. Agree?"

"Agree."

"So, do you mind if I tell you something?"

"As long as it is nothing to do with love or marriage, I am all ears."

"I trust you. I want you to know everything there is to know about me. I mean everything."

"Well, I can't think what that could be because I already know you don't change into a pumpkin at the stroke of midnight."

"No! I'm serious, Steve."

"Right. You'd better spill all then," Regan said with a smile. That smile was soon wiped from his face as he listened to Caroline.

"Okay but let me finish. Don't interrupt me, okay?"

"Okay, you got me intrigued now. What the fuck is it?"

Caroline used the remote control to mute the music.

"The thing is I have something to confess. It's something that if it ever comes out, I can wave goodbye to my career, becoming a judge and probably end up serving at least seven years in prison." Caroline shuddered, sighed and continued, "I have been using and dealing in cocaine for some time now. I knew it had to finish so I handed over the dealer and the business to another barrister, another coke head. But I am scared the truth will come out and I can't afford to let that happen."

Regan sat upright at one end of the sofa, taking in the scale of Caroline's confession, but remained silent. He studied Caroline's face while she spoke.

Over the next ten minutes Caroline unloaded her secrets while Regan sat and stared, showing no emotion. Monologue finished, Caroline said, "I needed to tell you. I hope you understand. I just can't keep all of this in. It's eating me away with worry."

There was a silence, not an awkward silence, just silence.

The quiet was broken by Caroline, "Well?"

"Well what?" Regan snapped.

"Why are you being aggressive?"

"I'm not. I just want to know what 'well' means."

"It means I want to hear what you think."

"I am shocked. I'm furious. It's bad enough you have a habit but dealing to barristers is pretty bad. For fuck's sake, you are supposed to be respected professionals; a part of society expected to uphold the rule of law. You are no better than the scum on the streets. There's no difference because you are all smart and use fancy words."

Regan heard his own words inside his mind. How could he ever think of going rogue? He was a law enforcement officer. He knew drugs and violence went hand in hand; they were inseparable like Siamese twins. Drugs ruined people's lives. In a flash, he knew who he was. More to the point, he knew drug dealing was not the solution to all the problems in his life. He had seen the precipice, experienced the temptation, and pulled back in time. Regan felt an inner relief.

"Caroline, you shouldn't have told me. I can't just forget it. I'm sorry."

"What! You going to inform on me? You can't do that! I got news earlier in the week my full-time appointment to Circuit Judge will come through any day now. I have worked so hard for this and I won't let anyone stand in my way."

Chapter 35

CAROLINE SEWELL'S FACE had lost all trace of a smile. Regan saw she had aged in front of his eyes when angered. He recalled the confrontation between Caroline and the barrister in the bar. Now he realised what the confrontation had been about and why she had threatened the other woman barrister. Regan was becoming angrier but held his counsel. They were supposed to be professionals but they flouted the law. He felt a compulsion to stay right where he was to weather the storm, take stock, and do what he was good at - infiltrating drug cartels. A cartel is a cartel no matter who they are, Regan thought. Besides, she was great in the sack. But no more foreplay or animal sex this night, mused Regan. He picked up his underpants from where Caroline had left them on the floor before he slipped them back on.

"Maybe it's better if I sleep on the sofa tonight," he said in a calm way, disguising his inner turmoil. Caroline ignored him and returned to the bedroom alone. She struggled to find sleep.

Caroline, for all her crass stupidity and compulsion to disclose all in telling Regan, knew how to survive. Regan was a threat. He could ruin everything she had worked so hard to achieve; her career could be ruined if the truth was out. Both pondered their next moves as they lay apart separated by not only a few yards but also by two different worlds.

SHE TOSSED AND TURNED in bed. Caroline thought, I must get rid of him, but how? I must kill him. Maybe I can hire a hit-man? There have to be guys in Brixton who will do it for a few scores of smack or cocaine. Too unreliable and could come back to me. I must do it, but how?

The following morning Regan and Caroline had coffee and toast as if nothing had happened. There was silence between them, not even a goodbye when Caroline left the flat. She collected her many briefs, instructions to defence counsel from an instructing solicitor, and letters from her chambers; one was marked with the official seal of the Lord Chancellor's Office. She ripped it open pulling out the letter. It was confirmation that she had been appointed a Circuit Judge sitting at the Crown Court at Canterbury. It was one of those days when she had no court work either as a barrister or as a part time judge. "Alright, listen up," she called out to the clerks, "lunch is on me."

It was a heavy drinking lunch finishing up at four in the afternoon. She called Regan, "Darling, great news. I got my confirmation letter. Come join us for more drinks."

"Where are you?" And more to the point what state are you in? You sound drunk."

"I plan to get even more drunk. Are you coming or not?"

"Yeah, but where are you?"

"We will be in the Pegasus Bar at Inner Temple."

Regan pondered much as he made his way to meet Caroline. He wondered why he was going at all because he knew things would never be the same again. He thought back to the loss of his wife and child. Regan then knew he had an issue dealing with loss.

On arrival at the bar, Regan again wondered why he had bothered. Nothing worse than a bunch of drunks when you are sober, he thought on surveying the scene in front of him. He was grateful that after a short time the debauchery was over. "Let's get a cab," Caroline slurred. Regan could see now what he was unable to see in the early stages of their relationship. She looked old and haggard when drunk or angry. Gone were the good looks of a woman who once appeared younger than her birth certificate.

Regan not only had trouble dealing with loss but was gallant. Regan made sure they got her back to the flat in a taxi despite his change in feelings towards Caroline. "Pour me a night cap, Steve," mumbled Caroline.

"Okay but the last. You have had enough already." Regan was prepared to placate her. He decided tomorrow was the end of their relationship. He was going to leave.

"Oh, fuck you. We aren't married and even if we were you don't give me orders."

"It's not an order. It's what's good for yourself. Besides, what about work tomorrow?"

"No work. I am taking it easy and having a lay in." Regan thought for a moment she had said 'shhlay inn.'

Caroline kicked off her shoes and was now relaxed on the sofa. Regan said, "Tell you what, I will go run a bath, then you will be ready for bed."

She scowled in response, an ugly scar of a frown, "There you go again. I will go to bed when I'm ready and on my own terms. You can be such a fucking pleb, Regan. Go have your bath and play with yourself in there."

"Oh, fuck off Caroline! You are one toffee-nosed prize bitch. Do you know that?"

A one-finger salute in Regan's direction was Caroline's mute reply.

Chapter 36

REGAN WAS SOAKING IN the suds when the bathroom door opened.

"Is that you? Come to join me now you have calmed down?" Regan wanted to suck those words back right from where they came from. It's over, he thought. He saw she was holding something. It had an electrical cord attached to it. Regan paled when he realised it was a portable electric space heater.

"What the fuck..."

Regan saw the power cord was plugged into an extension cable. He knew that must have been plugged into the mains in the hall. He knew he must leap from the bath but found he was unable to move a muscle. Still holding the heater in her hand Caroline turned to see Callum Colhoun. She also saw the knife he was holding.

"How the fuck did you get in here?"

"Simple. I memorised the combo for the punch keypad. You aren't as clever as you think, Cee. Should have changed it."

"Look, put that knife down. Be a good boy."

Callum roared like only a cocaine-fuelled crazed person can, "No way! I don't give a shit what happens to me. I am ruined. One of your dealers gave me up to the cops."

"What do you mean?"

"I fucked a tart on the game when I was in Sheffield. I gave her loads of charlie then she cried rape. She knew the dealer you gave me. The one on your list. He made sure the Bar Council knew all about the episode in Sheffield. The Bar Council have disbarred me and I'm looking at a minimum ten years jail time."

Regan now sensed the time had arrived. He made his move but Caroline heard the splash. She turned to face Regan who was still in the bathtub, water up to his waist. Both arms were stretched out on top of the sides of the tub ready to leap out. He levered himself up using his arms but one foot slipped on the bottom of the tub. Regan fell back into the soapy water with a shout of "Fuck!"

Caroline raised back her arm, still armed with the live electric heater as it was still plugged in to the extension cord and the mains. She was about to hurl the heater in the bath water when he struck. She felt a searing in her back right between her shoulder blades, forcing her into dropping the heater to the floor; wide-eyed she turned once more to face her attacker, Callum. It was all over for her within seconds. The Scottish barrister stabbed her time and time again in the chest, face, and neck in a frenzied attack. Caroline's blood spurted like a fountain from her neck and formed patches on the floor as she fell, first to her knees, then prone on to her face. She was dead.

Regan leaped out of the bath and ran towards Callum who dropped the knife and ran for the door to the flat. He fled. Regan started to run but slipped once more. He fell on to the slowly expanding greasy pool of blood emanating from the corpse.

"Shit!" Regan shouted as he looked in the hall mirror. He saw he was covered in Caroline's blood from his face right down to the soles of his bare feet.

"Fuck the protocols," he said to an empty flat. He knew he should have preserved the integrity of the crime scene but he felt both shocked and vulnerable owing to his nakedness. Before he got back in the bath water, he dialled 999.

"Police, please. Someone has been murdered."

Chapter 37

THE POLICE ARRIVED first in the form of uniformed officers then the cavalry. The local detectives turned up. Regan found himself being questioned.

"This isn't going to be easy for you to understand so first I suggest you call the Chief Superintendent to confirm my identity. I'm an undercover cop and she was a girlfriend."

Regan pointed to the prone lifeless body. "No, before you ask it wasn't me. It was a barrister. A Scottish guy called Callum. You can find out his full details by contacting the Sheffield CID. He raped a prostitute in that city."

Regan said no more. He remained tight lipped. The detectives had two options, to do as suggested or arrest Regan as a suspect. One of the brighter detectives saw the sense of making the call. He used the telephone in the flat and dialled a number.

"Yes, sir. I understand sir. Do nothing and wait but preserve the scene. Roger that, sir."

He turned to his colleagues and said, "Well you got the gist. We do nothing and preserve the scene. Apparently, the secret squirrel squad are on their way."

An hour passed before there was a buzz on the flat entry system. Five men were given access and walked into the flat.

Regan looked up on seeing them arrive and he beamed, "Red! How the fuck are you, me old mucker?"

"I'm fine, even if I am a bit 'armless.'" Red laughed at his own joke adding a, "Get it? Armless," and laughed loudly again.

"But what about you? Obviously, you can't cope without me."

"Me? I'm good. I'm still alive, aren't I? The crazy woman was gonna kill me before the crazy guy stabbed her to death."

Another man spoke. The tall, slender, older man with the close-cropped silver hair giving him the look of Lee Marvin. He had an air of authority, Regan thought.

"Hello, Steve, I'm Detective Chief Superintendent Graham. I am not at liberty to tell you who or what department I am attached to especially in front of the local guys. Let me deal with them first and I will come back to you. Just wait here."

Regan instantly liked him. He was calm and confident. He looked cool too in his black leather jacket.

Graham walked over to the local detectives huddled up near the front door of the flat. He spoke in hushed tones so Regan was unable to hear a thing. Whatever was said, the huddle disappeared with a collective tut and harrumph accompanied by the upwards 'whatever' eye motion.

The Lee Marvin lookalike with the air of authority walked with a confident gait. He gestured to Regan and Red to sit at the dining room table where he joined them. He spoke first, "Tom." A stout man with a shaven head turned to look in Graham's direction. He didn't reply but sat at the table.

"This is Tom Garner, he's a Detective Inspector but take no notice of ranks with us lot. We act as a team, work as a team and through me, we only answer to a senior Ministry of Defence minister, not a bloody civil servant but a politician."

Steve Regan sat up and paid attention. He was interested and respected this Graham, whoever he was. He decided to ask one early question because DCS Graham had said something unusual and interesting, "MOD? Why not the Home Office?"

"Wait, Steve. I will get to that if and when necessary."

Regan was again impressed.

"We are a secret undercover agency. Not just coppers but people drawn from the military and all walks of life. It's something I have been working on for years and only now have the top brass decided to give it a go. What I am about to say must go no further than these four walls, do you understand?"

Red said, "Yes, guvnor."

"No guvnor, no boss, no sir. Just first names, Okay?"

Red nodded.

Regan said, "I understand."

"Good. Are both you and Red interested in coming on board?"

Both men nodded their agreement.

"Great, because I have heard good things about you both."

"What about my arm?" Red asked.

"Don't worry about that just yet. Here's the thing. If you are in, then that's it. You have gone dark. You will be infiltrating some of the most dangerous organised crime gangs in the world. You will become disconnected from your forces, totally and utterly. No one, but no one, will know where you are or what you are doing except me, your handler, the MOD guy - if I choose to tell him, and this guy here or someone like him." Graham nodded towards a dark suited man who stood out owing to his diminutive, scrawny stature.

"Come here, please."

The tiny man approached, adjusting his glasses on the bridge of his nose. It seemed to be a nervous tic.

"You don't need to know his name. He and his team supply all the electronic surveillance stuff. They have access to gear you would never believe. Only the CIA and our special forces use it."

Tiny man spoke, "My name is unimportant but for the sake of social mores call me Jack. That isn't my real name."

Red and Regan both said, "Hi Jack!" with a smirk as it sounded like a Lebanese terrorist activity.

Jack solemnly replied, "Hello. I have something to tell you, Red. I know your father. I know him well. I saw him recently and he was telling me how proud he is of you. He went on to tell me about your accident and where you were in the hospital. It was me who told you Steve was in trouble."

"How do you know my father?" said Red.

"We knew each other as teenagers and he saved my life when some kids beat me up for being a scrawny weed. We have been friends ever since."

Regan interjected, "Next you will be telling me it was your Bonnie and you were the priest."

"Yes, and yes."

Red and Regan saw the funny side of the brief reply.

"You see, I am a frustrated undercover agent. I can't do what you guys do, but I see it and hear it. I'm watching you with all kinds of sophisticated kit."

"So you are the M and we are the 007's?"

All laughed until their bellies ached.

Chapter 38

THE LAUGHTER STOPPED as soon as DCS Graham spoke, "Here's what is going to happen. And it's a sign of what you are getting into, okay? This crime scene is going to disappear, wiped clean, as if it never happened..."

Regan's mouth opened wide, but no words would come out, but Red spoke, "And how the hell are you going to do that?"

"You heard about the CIA and removal teams?"

In awe, Regan said, "Yes."

"We have our own. They are better than anything the CIA has. Once I make my next phone call, this place will not bear witness to any crime, never mind murder."

Regan asked, "What about Callum? Is he going to get away Scot free with killing Caroline?"

"Yes. But why worry? He will end up serving about eight years in jail for the drug dealing, plus another seven for rape. This is the only way you, in particular, Regan, will live to fight crime another day. Not just any old crime but infiltrating the top echelons of organized crime gangs that affect the security of the United Kingdom. You and the other team members will be the cream of the cream. How does that grab you?"

"It grabs me a lot. I'm your man."

"And me," chimed Red.

"The best part is you will be paid handsomely."

"Now you are really talking my language. What exactly is handsome?" asked Regan.

"Four times your current salary and pensionable."

Red and Regan looked at each other. They high-fived, too excited to speak.

"I have another question," said Regan, "Can we recruit John Barnard?"

"Jack has told me all about him and the answer is 'yes.'"

DCS Graham made his phone call to the removal team.

Chapter 39

REGAN MADE HIS OWN call to John Barnard and arranged a meeting in the team's new office in an anonymous suburban house in South West London. It had the latest security gadgets monitoring twenty-four hours a day and also had the advantage of proximity to Heathrow. The team's brief was wide-ranging and was not restricted to operations on UK soil. If matters affected the security of the United Kingdom, Regan, Red, Barnard and any other future operative would fly to where they were needed anywhere in the world.

The safe house comprised of five ground floor rooms. One was an ops room with state-of-the-art electronic kit occupied by two personnel who worked a twelve-hour shift. They were then relieved by two other guys. The other rooms were offices and a kitchen cum dining area. There were five bedrooms, all kitted out with bunk beds. The half-acre of garden housed a separate nondescript building. It was a rest house comprising of a TV room, a library and kitted out with luxury leather Chesterfields.

Regan and Red went to the library after John had been formally inducted into the team. There, they chatted for a full hour.

Regan started the conversation between these two old friends, "I really can't believe all this. I am allowed to live to 'fight crime' another day, in another place. One time I didn't think this would ever happen." His eyes filled.

"I know what you are saying. You nearly went rogue, didn't you?"

"Red, me old mate, between you and me, yeah I did. How the fuck did you know?"

"Missus R told me. She knows you better than you know yourself. She said, 'Red, I am worried about him. I just know he is thinking of doing something terrible. I blame myself because I know he wants me to have the bloody operation.' I knew she was serious when she swore. Never heard your Mum swear before."

Regan's tears fell, trickling in warm rivulets down his cheeks. He held his hand aloft as if to stay any further conversation. Red took the hint and allowed Regan to regain control before he spoke again.

"Now for the good news, buddy, if you want some good news that is?"

"Shoot," Regan said with a smile.

"My father died leaving a lot of money to me. Part of it was savings and part from selling his house. Even though it was a tied house at one time, it fetched a lot because of its location in the Forest of Dean. So that means..."

"Don't say what I think you are going to say."

"I can say what the hell I want. It's my money. I'm sending you and your Mum to Boston for the operation she needs. Shut up ... that's not all. I'm coming too because I'm having a bionic arm fitted like the Six Million Dollar Man..."

"Oh, fuck off! You are teasing me."

"Not at all. I'm serious."

"Man! I love you," Regan said hugging Red.

"Steady fucking on. I'm not queer you know." Both hugged and laughed as one.

"Suppose I'd better call Ma and tell her the news."

"No need, she's already got her bags packed."

"Fucking A!" Regan and Red hugged again.

Chapter 40

REGAN, RED AND JOHN Barnard met in one of the rooms used as an office at the new team HQ. By now Graham had found a name for the team - DOCS. Red had asked what the acronym stood for, so Graham replied, "Destroy Organised Crime Syndicates."

The men made final arrangements to sort out the necessary paperwork. To Regan's relief, it was far less of a bureaucratic machination than anything the police could throw at him. New but false documents were provided for all three men. This was a new adventure with a new identity. A short time before business was concluded for the day, the phone rang. Regan answered it, "Yes?"

Jack's by now familiar voice was on the end of the line, "You and Red have an appointment with the DEA tomorrow at 10 am. Don't be late. Oh, and produce your new ID papers to security."

"Grosvenor Square?" Regan queried.

"Of course, where else? I forgot to tell you. Keep the Bonnie. Just take care of her."

It was 10 am exactly when Regan and Red were ushered inside the US Embassy by a uniformed Marine guard. He did not say one single word after inspecting their documents and checking the manifest affixed to a clipboard. A tall man approached them. He was wearing a long mackintosh. Regan was reminded of the Peter Sellers character Inspector Clouseau from the Pink Panther movie. 'Clouseau' hailed them in cheery fashion then ushered them into a suite of offices. The entrance door marked with a sign saying, 'Drug Enforcement Agency.'

There was a little small talk between the three men before 'Clouseau' left Regan and Red alone in a small office containing a table and three chairs. A brown folder marked 'Top Secret', was lying on the table. Regan opened the document folder which contained fifteen pages of official federal reports. He started to flick through them with Red alongside him as a second pair of eyes. Regan's eyes opened wide as the contents sank in.

Memories of Miami flooded back. He saw photographs of Enrico, Bill and Carlo. Regan scanned the text in a hurry. He let out a low whistle and said, "Enrico was an employee of Bill! Bill was the real boss."

Red looked puzzled. Regan carried on as if it was a running commentary, "Bill Morris, aka Guglielmo Di Maria, was a Mafia plant inside Customs with a view to infiltrating the DEA.

"Not only that but his real father was Don Galletti! He told me at Blue's cottage he'd only recently found out who his real father was."

Red asked, "What does it all mean?"

Regan replied, "It means it's outstanding they had the balls to infiltrate Customs. I'll tell you the whole story on the way to Boston. We have eight hours to kill on the flight."

Chapter 41

REGAN AND RED SAT NEXT to each other on the flight from Heathrow to Boston. Red's mother and John Barnard sat two rows behind. Red listened as Regan poured out the story. Once Regan had finished, Red said, "I missed it all because of my carelessness. You know what, Steve? I'm never going to touch a chainsaw again." The close friends laughed.

Red spoke again, "I need to ask you this, Steve."

Regan said, "Shoot! Whatever you want to know."

"About Caroline."

"What about her?"

"What on earth possessed you to stay with her after you found out what she was up to? Found out what she was really like."

"Man! I thought you knew me."

"That's no answer. Give!"

"I like danger. She was great in the sack. What else is there to know?"

"Yeah, okay, I know you well enough to buy that but..."

"But what? Buddy... "

"That last night. With her, I mean. For fuck's sake, Steve, you knew she was a crazy."

"Thought you knew me. I always see the best in people."

Regan smirked at Red. Red, using his remaining whole arm punched hard on Regan's shoulder.

The flight attendant saw the punch. She admonished Red and could not understand why his companion was laughing so loudly. Regan laughed more after Red told the attendant, "Don't mind me. I'm 'armless."

Regan sat sniggering with his hand covering his mouth. He gathered himself enough to say, "Guess that's your new punch line."

THE GROUP OF BRITISH subjects of Regan, his mother, Red, John Barnard plus three 'minders' who were special ops contractors vetted and hired by DCS Graham, settled into a pleasant Boston hotel for the third night of the trip. It was convenient to both hospitals scheduled to operate on Regan's mother's tumour and Red's arm. One of the minders took charge of driving the rented SUV as he was a trained escape driver. Regan and Red had given him a name – McQueen, owing to his expertise in driving.

McQueen parked the large red Chevrolet SUV on the side street next to the main entrance of the hospital where Red was to be operated on. Red had an appointment to meet his surgeon for a pre-operative check-up. Regan opened the front passenger door and placed both feet on the ground. He looked up at an approaching pick-up truck as it sounded its horn. The driver's window of the black truck powered down as it came level with Regan. The truck slowed so Regan was able to see the driver.

Regan heard the "whoop whoop" of a siren. It was a black and white Boston P.D. patrol car. A police officer hollered through a loudspeaker, "Sir, please move the car. You're in a tow-away zone." The black-and-white parked behind the Chevrolet SUV.

Regan blocked out the noise and kept looking at the driver of the black pick-up truck. The driver's arm extended from the open window. Regan saw it belonged to Carlo Vitale. He also saw the gun in Carlo's left hand. Carlo heard the cop too. He tossed the gun across to the front seat passenger. Carlo then pointed two fingers of his left hand at Regan. The undercover cop saw Carlo's mouth open and heard the sound, "Pop! Pop!"

As the black truck picked up speed, Regan heard Carlo shout, "You know who the fuck I am. Next time, Regan ... next time ..."

Regan turned to Red and said, "Get better soon buddy. We have work to do."

The End

Afterword

THIS BOOK IS THE FIRST in a trilogy featuring Steve Regan, undercover cop. Follow me on my website at www.stephenbentley.info for updates on all my new books.

I do hope you enjoyed this novella. My plan was to entertain you and set the scene for more danger and drama in the rest of the series. Perhaps Regan will find love to replace the wife and child he lost so tragically?

There are exciting times ahead for Regan, Red, and John Barnard. Don't miss the action!

If you enjoyed this story, please consider leaving a review on your favourite bookstore site. It need not be an essay! Just a few words will do. Think of it as a "tip" to an author in appreciation of his/her effort to entertain you.

You may subscribe to my monthly Readers' Club newsletter by clicking this link.[1]

---

1.   https://landing.mailerlite.com/webforms/landing/t4u2y9

Don't miss out!

Visit the website below and you can sign up to receive emails whenever Stephen Bentley publishes a new book. There's no charge and no obligation.

https://books2read.com/r/B-A-ZIWC-URSP

BOOKS 2 READ

Connecting independent readers to independent writers.

Did you love *Who The F*ck Am I?*? Then you should read *Dilemma*[2] by Stephen Bentley!

A STEVE REGAN UNDERCOVER COP THRILLER

DILEMMA

STEPHEN BENTLEY [3]

When you are undercover, many want to kill you.

Sicilian Mafia, Thai Mafia, even the CIA, they all want you dead.

Join undercover cop Regan in this emotion-packed roller coaster of a thriller.

Steve Regan is back and this time he's alone and undercover in a seedy area of Thailand on the trail of a Texan expatriate, Les Watkins, the biggest drug smuggler in South East Asia.Using himself as the bait, Regan attempts to score a $50,000 deal with the

---

2. https://books2read.com/u/49PEMX

3. https://books2read.com/u/49PEMX

Thai mafia in an effort to get closer to his target. As he finds himself embroiled deeper into the operation, Regan suspects Watkins may be connected to Regan's nemesis, ruthless Mafia boss Carlo Vitale, who has fled the United States following a triple bombing and assassination of three crime family heads. Besides staying alive, Regan has other problems when he suddenly finds himself facing the worst dilemma an undercover cop can face. **Dilemma is an edgy, suspenseful tale with twists and turns plus a sprinkle of romance.** *Though Book 2 in the Steve Regan Undercover Cop series, it can be read as a standalone book.*

Get it now.

Read more at https://linktr.ee/stephenbentley_author.

Also by Stephen Bentley

Steve Regan Undercover Cop Thrillers
The Secret: A Prequel to the Gripping Steve Regan Undercover
Cop Thrillers Series
Who The F*ck Am I?
Dilemma
Rivers of Blood

Standalone
How To Drive Like An Idiot In Bacolod: An Expat's Experiences
of Driving in the Philippines and How to Survive
The Steve Regan Undercover Cop Thrillers Trilogy
Comfort Zone: A Tale of Suspense

Watch for more at https://linktr.ee/stephenbentley_author.

About the Author

Stephen Bentley is a former police Detective Sergeant and barrister (trial attorney) from the UK. He is now a freelance writer and occasional HuffPost UK contributor on undercover policing and mental health issues.

His memoir 'Undercover: Operation Julie - The Inside Story' is a frank account of his undercover detective experiences during Operation Julie - an elite group of detectives who successfully investigated one of the world's largest drugs rings.

Stephen also writes fiction including the *Steve Regan Undercover Cop Thriller* and *Detective Matt Deal Thriller* series.

When he isn't writing, Stephen relaxes on the beaches of the Philippines with his family where he now lives.

Read more at https://linktr.ee/stephenbentley_author.

About the Publisher

Printed in Great Britain
by Amazon

32366208R00101